A Dose of Nice

A Parker Bell Florida Humorous Cozy Novel

A Dose of Nice

Parker Bell Humorous Mystery, Volume 1

Sharon E. Buck

Published by Southern Chick Lit, 2014.

This is a work of fiction. Similarities to real people, places, or events are entirely coincidental.

A DOSE OF NICE

First edition. February 1, 2014.

Copyright © 2014 Sharon E. Buck.

ISBN: 979-8223721932

Written by Sharon E. Buck.

Table of Contents

Sharon E. Buck

This a work of fiction. All characters appearing in this work are fictitious. Any resemblance to real persons, living or dead, is purely coincidental.

A Dose of Nice

Copyright © 2014 by Sharon E. Buck

All rights reserved. No part of this publication may be reproduced, distributed, or transmitted in any form or by any means, including photocopying, recording, or other electronic or mechanical methods, without the prior written permission of the publisher, except in the case of brief quotations embodied in critical reviews and certain other non-commercial uses permitted by copyright law.

CHAPTER ONE

Po'thole, Florida

It was the hottest day of the year... so far. Two hundred thousand hot, sweaty, stinky bodies were packed into a ten-block area in the small river town of Po'thole, Florida. They came to enjoy a vast array of handcrafted, not necessarily *handmade*, products found only at the Full Moon Crappie Festival held every Memorial Day weekend.

I'm Parker Bell, a Po'thole native, owner of a computer security consulting firm and national bestselling crime author, and, if you believe some of the locals, a turncoat who left Po'thole and River County for some twenty-seven years. Of course, I am now somewhat forgiven because I "had the good sense to come back home."

Uh, huh. I'm actually in Po'thole on business. Homeland Security apparently thinks there might be terrorists in the area and wants me to monitor a couple of businesses. My cover is that I'm here on vacation and just visiting friends.

Anyway, Main Street was lined with colorful popup tents filled with jams, homemade pickles, honey, and T-shirts in all shapes, sizes, and colors, straw hats with colorful bands, paintings exhibited by proud artists, and unusual, inexpensive products from Mexico and China. Each vendor had taken great care to arrange their wares so people could step into their tent, see everything, and then, hopefully, buy something.

Walking down the stretch of hotter-than-Hades asphalt, the smells of grilled sausage and peppers, kettle corn, fried fish, and, of course, steamed crab was so pervasive one was almost driven to buy something to eat.

Barbecue was not what came to mind for this particular weekend *nor* a murder. Po'thole hadn't had a murder in five years and why they had to have one the minute I arrived back in town is beyond me.

This particular weekend the devil apparently had taken his due and gave the good people of Po'thole a taste of what hell must be like. People were chugging fresh squeezed lemonade by the gallon and old people were fainting right and left. Wanna-be paramedics from the local community college used the Full Moon Crappie Festival as their required hands-on training class. The adult students were practically begging festival goers to have something happen to them. Faint, heart attack, heat stroke, they didn't care—they had credits they had to fulfill before graduation. The more accidents that happened, the more experience they received and the more they filled up their experience books for their classes.

It was bad enough that the little town of Po'thole was unfortunate enough to have a virtually unpronounceable name by anyone other than a native but to hear others struggle to say it was enough to cause gales of laughter from the townspeople. It was pronounced Po Ho by the natives or Pothole by those who lived north of Georgia. It was correctly pronounced *Poat Hole*, like goat hole, and was rumored to be an undefined Seminole Indian word with no apparent meaning. If you have ever driven through Po'thole, you would discover that it is truly full of potholes.

There wasn't one truly fit or healthy-looking person on the street. Fat women waddled down Main Street decked out in tank tops stretched over their protruding bellies, shorts that disappeared in the folds of loose flesh, and flip-flops. Most of the men had the dreaded Dunlop disease... their belly's done lopped over their belt. Unshaven, with a wad of chew in their cheeks, the men exuded the sexual attractiveness of pigs wallowing in the mud. And to think people didn't understand why I left this little piece of paradise.

Although the brochure produced by the local Chamber of Commerce showed a beautiful couple on the Victory Bridge gazing off into the haze (also known as the electric plant emissions from the power plant's cooling towers), the beautiful people apparently didn't bother coming to the Full Moon Crappie Festival.

As River County's citizenry strolled by the plate glass windows of where the Old Fashion Antique Show and Sale was being held, one of the out-of-town dealers commented it "was like watching a Sally-the-Swine parade."

A rather enthusiastic discussion of whether it was it really a Sally the Swine show or a Sally the Souse show ensued between the dealers. While the original comment was made near the noon hour, things escalated and continued through the cocktail hour which began at four o'clock in the afternoon. Obviously, the dealers were bored, and the antique sales were always slow on

Sunday but picked up again on Monday, however, they were beyond thrilled that they actually got to look out onto an open street as opposed to being cooped up in a smelly school gymnasium or some other structure that wouldn't allow fresh air or light in.

After living in big cities during that time "away from home," I have a somewhat jaded and cynical view of what denotes progress. Po'thole, contrary to the official view espoused by the aforementioned Chamber, isn't progressing very fast. In fact, you could say the turtle *died* in this race.

Downtown still had a few stores open. Many of the stores hadn't had a fresh coat of paint since the Civil War, and the old-timers insisted, rather loudly, that it was the gigantic super store on the outskirts of town that killed the shopping. However, where do you see these mouthy old-timers shop? Yep, you guessed it; at the gigantic super store they were complaining about.

The town is just as colorful as the folks who live there. I was happy to move away from Po'thole yet it seems like I got sucked back in for the Full Moon Crappie Festival.

I'm helping out Gracie Blanche, my best friend since fourth grade, in hosting the Old Fashion Antique Show and Sale. She heads it up and has been trying for years to get me to help her with it. I've always managed to stay far away during Memorial Day weekend. My idea of a vacation isn't to spend it in Po'thole during the hottest weekend of the year; however, when Homeland Security calls and requests that you visit hell in the summertime on a consulting assignment—and you need a plausible cover story—you don't have much choice in the matter.

Never would I have believed Gracie Blanche, a cute, petite, tiny thing of 4'10", could turn into Attila the Hun. While sweet to the antique dealers, she was a wee bit of a challenge to work with behind the scenes.

As head go-fer, my job was to help keep the dealers happy and do anything they needed to get done. Because I was bored silly, I started telling the dealers stories about Po'hole.

Gracie Blanche wasn't too thrilled that I was sharing the local gossip with out-of-towners. "After all," she sniffed, "we want them to come back. We don't need to be airing our dirty laundry."

That's one of the advantages and disadvantages of growing up in a small town. We all remember each other from way back when; the good, the bad, and the ugly. Personally, I've often wondered why no one ever sells errors and omission insurance for those outlandish stories from childhood. Most of the stories have been embellished so much that the truth, whatever version you choose to believe, is a mere wisp in the wind.

My mentioning to one of the dealers that the local minister's wife was having a fifth baby was an unpardonable sin. Apparently, Baptists don't have sex. Their babies are conceived by an appointment with the Divine and it's an immaculate conception.

Gracie Blanche moved me by the front door, hoping I wouldn't do any more damage to Po'thole's pristine reputation in the world.

As the owner of a computer security consulting firm, I was more than intimately acquainted with computers. I offered to help my friend by using my laptop to enter all of the potential customers' email addresses so they could receive antique email newsletters during the year. Never once did it occur to me that so many people visiting the Old Fashion Sale and Antique Show would be on a first name basis with Moses, and that they didn't have a computer.

Holding my laptop on my knees, I turned to speak to an old friend, and somehow, I swear I have no idea how it happened, a soft drink leapt up off the floor and spilled all over my laptop. My computer wasn't happy and decided it apparently no longer wanted anything to do with me. After much hissing, it died.

"Nooooooooooooooo," I screamed, jumping to my feet.

Gracie Blanche came running over when she heard my blood-curdling cry. Her dark brown eyes had the look of Attila the Hun on a mission.

"Parker, what did you do?"

"Ah, um, ah, my drink spilled all over my laptop and it died. I can't flipping believe it! I mean..."

"Stop! You didn't hurt anyone, did you?"

"Well, no, but I..."

"Forget about it. Pay attention to what the dealers want and don't annoy the customers."

Gracie Blanche can be mean.

Sulking from her remark, I called my office on my cell phone. I figured what the heck, they could just overnight me a new one.

"Triple T."

Good, it was Missy who answered the phone.

"Missy, hi, it's Parker and..."

"Let me guess." I heard a snicker in her voice. "You need a laptop overnighted?"

"Well, yes, but it wasn't my fault this time." I can't explain why I feel compelled to explain my computer accidents to my employees.

"Humph." Barely containing her giggles, Missy asked, "And how many laptops is that so far this year?"

This call was definitely not going in the direction I had planned.

"Um, I don't know. Three?" Sometimes things just happen.

"Parker..." My heart dropped at the mirth in my secretary's voice. "This is the fourth one this year and the second one in thirty days.

"You know, I think we could just put you in the Laptop-of-the-Month Club. You would receive a new one every thirty days and that way it would save you the *embarrassment* of having to call in."

I felt hot breath on the back of my head just before a solid *thunk* rattled my brains.

"Parker, all you have to do is pay attention to the dealers! Just do it!" I don't think that's what Nike had in mind when they came up with that slogan. Gracie Blanche just didn't understand how important computers are to our daily life.

Jimmy, the local town gossip, came barreling through the doors bypassing Miss Edna who was collecting the obligatory donation for the battered women's house. Miss Edna who was, to put it kindly, older than Methuselah, didn't appreciate this incredible lack of manners on his part.

Being the Southern lady that she was, she immediately sugar-coated her displeasure by drawling out, "Darlin', I'm sure you meant to pay the three-dollar donation on your way in."

Jimmy, who was tall, red-headed, skinny as a rail, and not the brightest bulb in the box, turned and focused his one straight eye at her.

"I ain't paying no donation to see old furniture and stuff!" Looking around to find an audience for his big announcement, he blurted, "Bobby's dead! The deputy said he's been murdered and I thought y'all might like to know about it!"

"Bobby" had once been the youngest mayor in the history of Po'thole and after two terms had decided to forego any future aspirations of climbing the political ladder. He had already built the largest beer store chain in Northeast Florida. The Beer Barn chain was a rousing success, particularly the local store.

Po'thole, located about halfway between the University of Florida in Gainesville and Crescent Beach, well, let's just say it was a natural stopping spot to tank up on a frothy liquid libation on that incredibly long and thirsty drive...all thirty-five minutes of it. The Beer Barn was set up so that one never had to leave their vehicle. Yep, you guessed it; it was a drive-through barn. All the customer had to do was place their beer order on one of those god-awful speaker phones like at any fast food restaurant, drive up to the first window, pay the cashier who was standing behind bullet-proof glass, pull forward to the next window and collect their beer. Bobby was immensely proud that he had streamlined the entire process of getting beer to the customer faster and, more importantly as a business owner, a way to cut down on beer being illegally adopted by both customers and employees.

Miss Edna, Gracie Blanche, and I all gasped at the same time. The antique dealers, not knowing who Bobby was and, honestly, not giving a rat's pa-tootie about him, were, however, curious about the circumstances of his death.

Worth Earlington, (what could possibly be a better name for a gay antique dealer than that,) asked the obvious. "Who did it and what for? Was it a love triangle?"

Jimmy, eyeing Worth quizzically, said, "Well, he wasn't...I don't know what you mean by that."

We all stifled snickers.

"Honey, would you like a cup of tea to calm your nerves?" Bless Miss Edna's heart, she was sure that a cup of hot tea would cure almost any problem or social ill.

I whispered to Gracie Blanche, "He needs to shake hands with Jack Daniels, I bet." Gracie Blanche, although vertically challenged, could still reach the back of my head and swatted it this time with an open hand. "You are going to get me in trouble." I felt a headache coming on. Being popped in the back of the head twice before noon didn't help matters any.

Jimmy looked at Miss Edna as if she had lost her marbles.

"Listen, here, I came in to tell y'all about Bobby." Jimmy was a little indignant he had been interrupted. "You know Bobby's weekend getaway place upta Bostwick on the river? Well, Dewitt got a phone call, someone asked for him personally, saying that he might want to check out Bobby's place 'cas he might find something interesting up there. And, oh, yeah, he needed to be out there by 10 a.m. As I understand it, Dewitt wasn't any too happy about having to miss going fishing and all.

"Anyway, Dewitt took one of the new deputies with him up there. The gate was already open and the pit was smoking. Apparently, whoever did Bobby in decided he needed to be barbequed."

Before Gracie Blanche could stop me, my mouth opened and the words flew out all on their own. "I hope they used the smoking sweet sauce."

Well, the dealers almost fell on the floor, they were laughing so hard. Miss Edna did not appear to be amused by my remark and Gracie Blanche, well, let's just say I probably won't be working the Old Fashion Antique Show and Sale next year. *Thank you, Lord! Thank you, Jesus!*

Jimmy, on the other hand, said, "Well, Parker, I'm not sure what kind of sauce they had on him but I do know it wasn't any of that Carolina mustard crap."

Of course, that just made me and the dealers laugh all the louder. Tears were streaming down our faces. Gracie Blanche couldn't hold her laughter in any more. Miss Edna finally cracked a smile.

"Jimmy, tell us what Dewitt found out," Gracie Blanche finally spluttered between her tears.

He nodded knowingly. "Dewitt said the new deputy probably wasn't going to make it much longer. He threw up. Bobby apparently had been shot in the back of the head and then had been trussed up on a spit over the fire."

"Oh, mercy, mercy," murmured Miss Edna. "His mama does not need to know that."

"Jimmy, who does Dewitt think did it?"

"Well, Gracie Blanche, he don't know. In fact, he's real upset. He had just seen Bobby on Thursday night. They had been exercising together."

Worth, catching on quickly to the ways of River County and with a twinkle in his eye, asked, "Bending elbows?"

Jimmy shook his head. "They was drinking."

"How long has Bobby been dead?"

"Gracie Blanche," Jimmy said, obviously starting to get a wee bit annoyed. "I have done told you everything I know except that it will probably be in the mullet wrapper tomorrow."

"Today is Sunday and the paper won't come out again until Tuesday," I said.

The local newspaper several years ago had decided in its infinite wisdom to discontinue printing the paper Monday through Friday. Why? Because they had hired a consulting group out of Jacksonville to conduct a survey to see how many folks wanted to read about how the local football team did on Friday night and they wanted to read about it Saturday morning.

In short, they didn't want to wait until Monday morning to see how the county teams fared. While it was heavily rumored that only one-hundred people had participated in the survey, and all of those were former local football players, the paper changed its publishing schedule. Those guys were probably trying to hang onto their glory days, I surmised. Nevertheless, the paper now was printed Tuesday through Saturday.

Gracie Blanche turned to me. "Regardless, it's still going to be in the newspaper."

"Well, Jimmy, what are the details?"

Jimmy, bless his heart, didn't have the sense God gave a goose. "They had women upta the camp! Dewitt's trying to figure out who they was and where they got off to."

Gracie Blanche fixed those dark brown eyes on me, drew up to her full 4'10" self, and said, "Parker, since you're on *vacation*, you don't need to get involved."

"What would make you think I want to get involved in a local murder?" I was indignant that she would even think I wanted to be part this. "Since I've been gone forever and three days and I only know Bobby from way back in the day, I can't imagine any reason why I would be remotely involved with this."

Jimmy blurted out, "Yeah, but you know a lot. You been writing about those true crime stories."

I blushed. Heck, I was impressed that Jimmy could read, what with his having only one eye and all. He had me there. However, I didn't think a single murder in a small, sleepy Southern town would have much national interest. I was wrong.

CHAPTER TWO

Bobby

The stories of Bobby Derlicter are the stuff legends were made of. He'd been a super jock during high school.

During the annual "smash 'em" event where a junked car, supplied by the local car dealership and written off at full face value for tax purposes, was pummeled with a twenty-pound sledgehammer by the seniors. For some unknown reason, this was supposed to fire up the football team into a frenzy so they would win the first game of the season.

Think about it, what high school coach in his right mind would ever schedule a tough team for the first game?

Bobby, being the super jock that he was, on the very first swing slammed the sledgehammer through the roof of the car. Turning to the crowd of apparently swooning girls, he generously offered to let one of the girls take a swing at the car.

In Bobby's world, a female could not possibly be as good as he was at anything. In fact, although politically incorrect—and in a small town who cares about political correctness in high school—Bobby had been known to say that right out loud, in front of girls no less.

A small group of girls took umbrage at his remarks and decided it was time Bobby understood what the word "equal" meant. They asked one of the female weightlifters to take a turn at the car and show Bobby that females were every bit as "equal" as he was.

Svetlana, new to the United States and Po'hole via the Ukraine, would never win a beauty contest, and due to her strenuous weight training schedule, weighed almost as Bobby. Her coach emphasized later that Svetlana did not partake or use steroids of any type; she was just naturally large and exceptionally strong for her age. No one believed that for a minute, but that was their story and they stuck to it.

The sledgehammer was next to the car, head down with the handle standing straight up in the air. Svetlana dragged it back a few feet with one hand, looked over her shoulder at Bobby and shouted, "Power to the women!" The crowd standing near Bobby snickered.

Svetlana grabbed the handle with the fury and intensity of being in a weightlifting competition, and lifted it up and over her shoulder in one smooth, primal, fluid motion. That hammer came down on the hood of the card with the power of a runaway train. She didn't just put a dent in the hood of the car, the hammer went all the way through the hood and into the engine block where it lodged with the handle standing at attention.

The crowd was frozen with the sheer enormity of what had just happened.

Svetlana? Well, she turned to the now silent group, raised her arms in victory, and screamed, "Power to the women!" Bobby just stood there, eyes bugging out of his head.

She turned back to the car and jerked the hammer out, lifting up half the engine block before it was freed. It flew back over her shoulder, bounced up once, took aim at Bobby's knee, and decided to kiss it.

You could have heard Bobby's scream clear over to Crescent Beach some thirty miles away.

The clean and jerk exhibition of the hammer broke Bobby's leg just above his knee effectively ending his chances at any college or pro career. He wasn't a happy camper the rest of his senior year.

The girls who had orchestrated Svetlana's demonstration of feminine power were beyond happy that she had out-powered the guys on the pounding of the car. They didn't care much about Bobby's broken leg.

You ask how I know so much detail about this incident? Well, now that the Statute of Limitations has expired and Bobby's dead, I will cheerfully admit that I was one of the five girls who convinced, (coerced might be a better word,) Svetlana into showing off her strength with the hammer. That was a good day in high school. There weren't that many of them for those of us who weren't the "in" group. We celebrated at the local Dairy Queen.

And where is Svetlana these days? Last any of us heard, she was coaching the U.S. Women's Weightlifting Team. Apparently she had such a good time with the hammer and the car, it's now been indoctrinated into the United States training program.

Who said glasnost is dead?

Bobby wasn't fit to live with during his senior year. Of course, after four surgeries, no college football scholarship, and finding out he was going to be a daddy...three times, no less, who could blame him for being a wee bit cranky?

Bobby bragged to his buddies on the football team that he had bagged three virgins. Apparently the three girls were adoring fans of Bobby's and when he suggested a party in a motel room complete with a bottle of Cold Duck, how could they possibly resist the charm of a football star? It was Bobby's version of Girls Gone Wild.

Later, when Bobby denied to his daddy, a really bad and stupid thing to do, that the babies couldn't possibly be his, Big Bob believed him. That is until the girls took Bobby to court and told the judge, the Honorable Joseph Paul Hungert, that Bobby had told them they couldn't get pregnant the first time and, no, he wasn't going to wear a condom because, "it interfered with his pleasure."

The Honorable Joseph Paul Hungert was an elder at the First Presbyterian Church of Po'thole, a well-respected judge, and Bobby wasn't the first football player he had seen in his courtroom. He absolutely detested football players who thought they were above the law. He graduated magna cum laude from the University of Florida Law School and had his choice of well-paying jobs elsewhere. Why he chose to come back to here is beyond me. Obviously, I don't appreciate the finer points of living in a small town.

He listened to the girls' story, and while he doubted they were as innocent as they wanted him to believe, he did believe they were pregnant and so ordered a DNA test. He also ordered Bobby to pay for it.

The DNA results came back six weeks later. Apparently, it was an ugly, ugly scene in the courtroom.

The Honorable Joseph Paul Hungert said privately later if he knew how to write a movie script, he would make a fortune with everything that happened in his courtroom that day. Sadly, he didn't think anyone would believe it.

According to my inside source, Mr. Tommy the court bailiff, the Honorable Joseph Paul Hungert entered the courtroom and asked for the paternity test envelopes. All three girls were there along with their mothers. Bobby was there, grinning and winking at everyone like he didn't have a care in the world. Big Bob was also there, and having to take a day off from work without pay, he wasn't the same ray of sunshine his son was.

The Honorable Judge cleared his throat after carefully re-reading the DNA results. "Mr. Derlicter, please stand."

Bobby stood up, still grinning.

"Mr. Derlicter, these papers," he held them up, "state conclusively that you are the father of each of these girls' babies and although you are in high school, I am ordering you to pay $50 a week per child, until such time as you secure a meaningful full-time job. That is $150 per week, assuming no one has twins or triplets, until you are twenty-one years of age, or you receive a four year college degree. At that time, you will come back before the court and child support will be based upon the income you will receive in your new job."

Bobby, still smiling, piped up. "Your Honor, it's okay. Two of the girls are going to have an abortion. I'm paying for them and..."

All hell broke loose in the courtroom, according to Mr. Tommy.

The mothers of the girls started to shout, "Unt un, my child ain't having no abortion!" "No, she's not!" And, apparently, the only money motivated mom of the three, shouted out, "I want a cash settlement! Forget the darned abortion!"

Bobby was swollen up with pride and ego. He thought he had everything figured out. He was wrong.

Big Bob, sitting behind Bobby, yanked his oh-so-ugly-he's-cute son around, looked him square in the eye, and punched him in the jaw. Mr. Tommy said it sounded just like a 22 rifle shot. Bobby fell back against the table unconscious. Apparently, Big Bob didn't share Bobby's same sense of humor or priorities.

Mr. Tommy, former world famous alligator wrestler and being at least two-hundred pounds overweight, just sat down and started to laugh at the comical scene. The girls were all shouting at their mothers and the mothers were shouting back at the girls.

Mr. Tommy almost lost his state pension over the incident. He was laughing so hard that he started to roll off the chair. The chair, unfortunately, wasn't designed to handle that much weight on just two legs. It collapsed under Mr. Tommy.

The ruckus escalated when the Honorable Joseph Paul Hungert hit the panic button under his desk. It had never been used and the sheriff's department wasn't exactly sure what they were supposed to do when the call came in. Since the SWAT team was running drills that day, and as luck would have it they were only two blocks away, they took charge and rushed over to the courtroom.

They came charging through the doors, shields up, guns pointed, ready to toss tear gas at the offenders and thus saving the world from an unconscious football star, screaming teenage girls, and their shrieking mamas. The Honorable Joseph Paul Hungert jumped up so quickly when the Po'thole storm troopers came rushing to save him that his chair rolled across one of the corners of his official judge's robe, thereby snapping his head back in his haste to escape from the lunacy of his formerly calm courtroom.

Mr. Tommy said the Honorable Joseph Paul Hungert let out an awful sound. He couldn't decide if the judge was trying to yell for help or if he was actually dying of a heart attack.

Bobby said later that his senior year in high school defined the rest of his life.

No other girls ever got pregnant; Bobby never went to college or got married. While he was a big boy in high school, he gained almost fifty additional pounds within two months after graduation.

Now that he was eighteen and of legal drinking age, he consumed as much beer as possible. Sitting in the back of a pickup one hot and humid night, popping open another can of Coors Light, Bobby groused to his buddies that he was tired of having to visit two or more convenience stores every night to get enough *cold* beer to drink. Bobby would only drink Coors Light.

Bobby's dream was a beer barn stocked with cold beer all the time. His buddies all laughed and basically made fun of him.

Suffering from a huge hangover and barely being able to see one morning, Bobby thought his idea might have some merit. He went over to East Po'thole, looked over a closed fast food restaurant and called the realtor's number on the sign.

While waiting on a call back, he wandered over to the convenience store next door and flirted with the girl on duty before asking, "Who's the beer distributor and how do I contact them?"

The girl, smiling and blushing through all of Bobby's banter, gave him every distributor's phone number and sales rep's name.

Bobby figured he was on a roll and called the Coors sales rep. He met Bobby within the hour. No other sales rep returned Bobby's call that day.

He called the realtor again and left another message. This one was a little more to the point. "If you want to rent this rattletrap place in the next 24 hours, call me. If not, I'll get me somebody else."

The realtor called back in twenty minutes.

Bobby had had a credit card since he was fifteen and the limit on it was now fifteen-thousand dollars. For all of Bobby's other faults, he was good at handling his money.

Within thirty days, Bobby had renovated the fast food restaurant into a drive-through Beer Barn, had rented three outdoor signs, complete with buxom blonde and a can of Coors Light in hand, between Gainesville and Po'thole. Those signs said, "Thirsty? Visit the Beer Barn on the way to the beach."

Bobby turned out to be very resourceful and an excellent businessman. Who knew? By the time he was twenty-one he owned a chain of Beer Barns and was a multi-millionaire several times over.

What happened to his original Coors sales representative Joey Jones? He ended up working for Bobby and, as it turns out, he was also an excellent businessman. His area of expertise was, what else, negotiating beer prices with the various distributors.

Joey was having drinks one night at a local watering hole and was drinking, of course, his favorite liquid libation Coors Light. He and Bobby considered it nectar of the gods.

Joey had a friendly rivalry going with all of the beer reps. They swapped old war stories about various places they sold beer and Joey always joked about how the Beer Barns sold the most Coors Light in the entire South— a noble accomplishment and one he was immensely proud of.

The Budweiser sales rep was also quaffing down his brand across the bar from Joey. Apparently he had consumed several more beers than Joey when he yelled across the bar, "Hey, you guys couldn't stay open a week if you didn't carry our beer in your stores."

The Bud rep was quite sure Joey hadn't heard him so he walked over and loudly said, "You guys couldn't stay open a week without our beer. Everyone knows the number one beer in America is Bud."

Joey smiled. "Okay, let me buy you a beer."

The poor fellow didn't have a lick of sense. "Did you hear me? I said..."

"Yeah, I heard it. I don't believe it but I heard you."

"You and Bobby think you know everything. Well, you don't..."

Wrong thing to say to the man who buys your products. Joey never said a word to the guy, pulled his wallet out, slapped his money down on the bar, and walked out. His buddies all looked at each other, rolled their eyes, and told the Bud man he had just stepped in a snake pit.

"Yeah, yeah, yeah. We're still number one in the country and he's not." Consuming too much alcohol can have a disastrous effect on one's career.

The next day all thirty-two Beer Barns had a fax waiting on them when they arrived at work. It read, "Until further notice no purchases or deliveries of Budweiser products are authorized. This includes any deliveries scheduled for today. Double your Coors order. Sandra will be faxing you new price points."

The managers were burning up the telephone lines in minutes trying to figure out what was going on.

The Bud delivery guys weren't too happy either. They ended up taking all of the deliveries back to their warehouses.

It took about two hours before Joey received his first phone call from an irate sales rep. "What do you mean you're refusing our products? We're Budweiser, you can't do that!"

Joey asked, "Who's your customer?"

The poor fellow obviously wasn't thinking clearly when he answered, "Why, the working man, of course."

Joey laughed. "Wrong. It's me, the Beer Barn, and we don't have to carry your products now or ever. Goodbye." He slammed the phone down just as Bobby came through the door.

Over the next two weeks Joey and Bobby refused to take any of the Budweiser phone calls or to see them when they showed up unannounced in the lobby. And Joey, *oops*, just happened to let one of the reporters from the local newspaper in on what was going on.

Well, the national wire services picked up the story on the beer wars and the next thing everyone knew was that Bobby, the Beer Barn, and Po'thole were splashed all across the TV news and entertainment channels.

Bobby equated this as David versus Goliath. He was David and the big mean corporation was Goliath. By golly, no one was going to tell him what he had to buy for his stores. He was an American and he had free choice. Why it said so right in the Constitution...somewhere.

The Coors people absolutely loved Bobby and all of the free publicity they were getting. The City of Po'thole was thrilled they were getting good, positive publicity for the town. Beer Barn sales exploded. And the Bud folks were downing aspirin like it was going out of style over their ever-increasing, public relations nightmare.

Bobby, being the brilliant marketer that he was, managed to keep the beer war going for three weeks on the national news.

Sales skyrocketed and because of all the publicity and interest in the Beer Barn concept, Bobby started franchising his idea born in the back of a pickup truck on a hot August night.

He required all new franchisees to come to Po'thole for their training. Hotel and food sales increased fairly dramatically in a very short period of time. The townspeople loved Bobby and what he did for the local economy.

Then they started talking about Bobby running for mayor. Bobby thought that was a hoot, him being in his early twenties and all.

Then he had an epiphany. What if he had Budweiser donate a new children's park to the city, thus giving them very favorable publicity, and he, Bobby, being so moved by their generosity to his hometown, would let them back into his stores?

Of course, Bobby wouldn't know up front about the wonderful new park that they were donating nor would he know that they were going to throw him a very extravagant, (by Po'thole standards anyway,) campaign fundraiser for his mayoral run six weeks after the beer war ended.

The deal was struck behind closed doors over the phone and that's how Bobby Derlicter became Po'thole's youngest mayor at the age of twenty-two.

After his stint as mayor, he continued to do what he did best, drank vast quantities of his favorite liquid foamy libation, hung out with the guys at his hunting camp, swapped lies, told tall tales, and made money hand over fist.

He was just basically a good ol' boy who found a way to make lots of money and have fun. He was generous to the various civic organizations in town, although he could be quite patronizing to some of the women's groups. The Lady Gatorettes hated him.

That's why it was such a surprise to the town to find Bobby trussed up and found swinging over an open Bar-B-Q pit at his hunting camp. Who could possibly have hated Bobby enough to kill him? Even in the South, barbeque redneck would probably not be a big seller *regardless* of the type of sauce.

There were twelve empty Coors bottles next to the fire pit. At least, Bobby died with his favorite beer nearby. After all, what goes better with barbeque than a Coors?

CHAPTER THREE

Dewitt

"Squirrels in heaven, squirrels in heaven, squirrels in heaven, and I hope you are there too, Bobby," muttered the sheriff to the empty unmarked car. Things couldn't have fallen apart at a worse time.

Sheriff Dewitt Munster had been the sheriff of River County for eleven and a half years and he was up for re-election in six months. This would make the third time he had to run against an opponent.

His predecessor, the much beloved Allen Walters, had assured him that after he ran the first time it would be a piece of cake to get re-elected up until the time he wanted to retire. After all, Walters had been re-elected ten times with virtually *no* opposition.

But apparently Sheriff Munster wasn't as beloved as Allen Walters had been. Each time that he'd run, he'd only won by the slimmest of margins. It was darn discouraging not to mention humiliating to win an election by only six votes particularly since the local "alleged" drug dealer had almost beaten him in the last election.

"Yessiree, Bobby Derlicter, I take your murder very personally."

******

Being that Po'thole only had one coffee shop in town and the fastest way to catch up on the local gossip was to get your coffee there, I made a daily pilgrimage to the coffee mecca.

I wasn't paying the slightest bit of attention while standing in line. I'm almost comatose first thing in the morning and coffee does help to jumpstart my batteries. Otherwise, I turn into a really mean and nasty person. Unfortunately, there are those in two different parts of the country who say I'm like that even *with* coffee. I try not to associate with them.

Dewitt, ever the observant individual, turned and spotted me standing behind him in line.

"Oh, hey, Parker. When did you get back into town? Who are you visiting now?"

I always really had to force myself to remember to call him Dewitt and not Dimwit. His nickname in school was Dimwit Monster. Without that first cup of coffee, I didn't want to risk making a political blunder so early in the morning.

"Well, Big D," I said, figuring he'd like being called that, "I'm just kind of in town for a brief moment in time."

"What brings you back?"

While I can be a real Chatty Cathy later in the day, without that first cup of coffee in the morning, well, let's just say my social skills are a little lacking.

"Do what?" Oh, yeah, my vocabulary isn't particularly abundant either.

"I said what brings you back to town?"

I was pretty sure my saying "the coffee" wasn't going to be well received.

"I just came back for a little R&R."

Wrong thing to say to a law enforcement officer in a small, sleepy Southern town where the streets roll up at night.

"Here?" Suspicion crossed his face. "This is about as quiet a place as you could ever find. No one goes out at night here. I thought you liked the big cities. Don't you live in Atlanta?"

Please, I *really* needed coffee. The girls behind the counter were moving slower than cows going to a slaughterhouse. Why was Dimwit flapping his lips and expecting an intelligent answer from me?

"I came down because Gracie Blanche wore me down on helping her with the antique show thing."

Dewitt sort of smiled. "Yeah, she can be somewhat on the persuasive side." He looked at me carefully. "You've written three best-selling crime books, right?"

I nodded. My head was starting to throb and my eyes weren't focusing too well either. I *desperately* needed coffee. I could feel the coffee demons attacking my caffeine-starved body.

Dewitt looked at me sourly. "You're not going to write about this murder, are you?"

Where are those girls and the darn coffee?

"Well, let's put it this way..." I paused for effect. "No."

"I'll bet you worked pretty closely with law enforcement on your books, didn't you?"

I knew Dewitt wanted something. He usually wasn't at all talkative. In fact, he rarely said much of anything. When did he turn into the Po'thole's equivalent of Chatty Cathy? I felt my entire being sinking into the bottoms of my dirty sneakers.

"Sometimes."

I could feel myself starting to say the coffee-drinkers prayer. "*God, please let me have coffee right now. I promise I won't kill anyone to get it. I thank you for my cup of coffee right now.*"

If I was ever kidnapped and they wanted me to talk, all anyone would have to do is withhold coffee from me, particularly first thing in the morning. I would fold like a bad umbrella and tell them everything.

"Don't you do something else besides write?" he asked as he poured an unbelievable amount of sugar into the large Styrofoam cup.

Although I was annoyed that Dimwit couldn't believe someone could actually make a living writing, it did provide me with the much needed change of subjects.

"Yes, I own a computer security consulting firm."

"You doing well enough to take a vacation, huh? Pretty good. I don't even take a vacation," Dewitt muttered at me.

"I've got good people, it lets me travel, I do some computer consulting for the companies who need their computer systems protected against the hackers." *Where was my darn coffee?*

Dewitt looked at me curiously.

"Work with the FBI and law enforcement agencies all across the U.S., right?"

Since our Homeland Security work was pretty much confidential, I didn't plan to elaborate for Dimwit. "Yep."

He smiled and grinned with his coffee-stained teeth. "Great, why don't you swing by the office in about an hour and take a look at our equipment?"

Bam! I swear I should have seen it coming but nooo, that slow girl hadn't even *taken* my coffee order yet, and I just wasn't awake. I vaguely wondered if there was a special place for me on the Zombie planet.

"Dim, er, Dewitt, I am not really a hardware person. If you have something wrong with your computers, call the company who sold them to you." I glanced over at the register where the order-taker should have been standing.

Now that silly girl stood ready to take my order, pencil in hand.

"Black," I snapped.

She looked at me bug-eyed. She must have had a long night.

"Huh?"

"I said I want a black coffee. The largest one you have."

"Nuttin' else?"

"Nope." I turned back to Dewitt, closed my eyes, and took a deep breath. "Big D, I'm taking a break right now and...."

"Criminals don't take breaks."

"Yeah, I understand that, but I didn't come back to here to work. I just came back to take a break."

Sheriff Munster grinned again, totally ignoring my comments. "Great! See you in an hour." And he walked out the door.

I was flabbergasted. My coffee was sitting on the counter when I turned back around. Why couldn't they have gotten Dewitt's coffee that fast? This whole conversation would have never happened. "Did you hear that?"

The girl just looked at me. "You said you wanted it black. Do you or don't you?"

I just shook my head. I was back in Po'thole all right. If you can multi-task, don't come here. Your talent's wasted.

About that time, Lucy Lu burst through the door. Before going any further, let me provide the color commentary on Lucy Lu. Well, okay, it's really gossip, but it is funny.

Patsy Lu, Lucy Lu's mother, has been known to add a wee bit of liquid libation to whatever pot of something she was cooking. Her favorite liquid libation to use is Jack Black. Of course, I guess if I had six kids all with the middle name of Lu, I might resort to doing the same thing.

Donald Duck, Lucy Lu's daddy, yes, his mama really *did* name him that because she loved Walt Disney and wanted to pay homage to the great man. Anyway, Donald ran off years ago with a Jenna Lou, but not before he had sired six kids all with the middle name of Lu, with Patsy. At least, they didn't name the kids after the seven dwarfs.

Patsy Lu Duck was truly convinced the reason why Donald insisted each child have the middle name of Lu was so that she would be forever tormented when she called them.

Everyone in the world, okay only in Po'thole, reminded her that *her* middle name was LU and each child spelled her name LU not LOU. Patsy Lu was not convinced that Donald had insisted on the middle name of Lu out of his love and devotion to her, particularly after she found out that he had been having an affair with Jenna Lou.

It was shortly after Donald Duck ran off with Jenna Lou that Patsy Lu started to add her special liquid ingredient when she cooked. The kids loved it.

In fact, they loved it so much they started taking it to school for their lunch.

Never let it be said that Patsy Lu's children weren't innovative and had an entrepreneurial bent. They, all six of the Ducks—Tommie Lu, Peggy Lu, Lucy Lu, Wendy Lu, Layla Lu, and Mona Lu, were fairly enterprising at an early age. They sold their lunches to other kids.

The kids who purchased the lunches became very slap happy during lunch and then wanted to snooze during the afternoon classes.

The teachers, beyond thrilled that they had one less rowdy child making noises in the classroom, apparently didn't notice for months that the Lu sisters' lunches contained a powerful liquid concoction. What gave the secret away was that Mona Lu snatched up all of her sisters' lunches one day and sold them first, not realizing that Patsy Lu was so delighted that her children were scarfing up her meals that she had added even more of her special secret ingredient.

The children were so happy that day that they shared their lunch with other students. Instead of going to sleep like they normally did, their afternoon classes turned into Happy Hour...complete with cherry bombs going off in the girls and boys bathrooms...three times.

One teacher was heard to comment, "I didn't sign up to teach in a war zone and I'm not doing it now!" However, since she was a tenured teacher, she decided she could hang in there for another year before she retired.

Patsy Lu was called into the principal's office regarding her enterprising children. Now, Patsy Lu might not have been the best mother in the world but she did love her children and their loving her cooking so much that they chose to share it and make money from it with others just warmed the cockles of her heart. She was immensely proud of this and to have some principal tell her...tell her...that her children couldn't bring the nourishment that a good home-cooked meal provided them was insulting.

She let loose on the principal and let all out of the venom she had been storing up since Donald left her for Jenna Lou. She blasted the principal so far into the middle of next week that he later said he thought there had been a nuclear attack in Florida and that only he, unfortunately, survived with Patsy Lu.

Upon giving it some additional thought, meaning he needed to get the crazy woman out of his office, he agreed he might have acted in haste and the kids were free to continue to bring lunches from home. He did ask her to cut back, just a little, on the Jack Black.

Apparently Patsy Lu had some photos of him and her next door neighbor doing a little more than having a parent-teacher meeting. She might have mentioned that during her tirade which is quite possibly the reason he was so willing to let the kids continue to bring their homemade lunches.

Coming through the coffee shop's door, Lucy Lu had the energy of a runaway freight train. I vaguely wondered what she needed coffee for since she was already overly stimulated.

She was about as big around as she was tall—and she stopped right in front of me. *Oh no, not another conversation....*

"Why, Parker Bell, what are you doing in Po'thole? Did you hear about Bobby Derlicter? What are you doing here? Are you coming to the Ladies Circle meeting tomorrow?"

Dear God, the woman sounded like she was on speed, she was speaking so fast. Heck, if I didn't know any better I'd say she sounded like she came from New York City which was the ultimate *curse* in Po'thole.

"Whoa, Lucy Lu! Breathe, girl, breathe!" I was starting to wonder if I'd survive my forced visit. "As to your first question, I'm just coming back for a while. Get away from...."

"The big city life," she finished for me. "I knew it, I knew it! I knew you would come back to what little sense you have and come back home!" The only way to describe the deluded woman's expression was gleeful.

I felt a migraine coming on and it wasn't even 9 a.m. yet. The coffee wasn't giving me the kick start I needed on what was shaping up to be a lousy day. And here I was thinking it was going to *fun* being back in Po'thole.

"No, Lucy Lu, I came back because..."

"You have a broken heart from when you and Joe D. broke up, you've never found another man like him, and you came back for him. I knew it!" Her eyes positively sparkled at the thought.

I, on the other hand, felt my stomach drop and the pain of a heart ache. I had loved Joe D. at one time but I wanted more out of life than being the wife of "We Make Money, CPAs". He never could understand why that wasn't good enough for me.

I didn't wish to encourage Lucy Lu along her line of faulty reasoning.

"When and where is the Ladies Circle meeting?"

Lucy Lu took a step back like I had slapped her. "Well, Parker, it's the same place and time it's always been. Ten o'clock at the church hall." She eyed me like she would the devil if he had had the bad sense to confront her. "I forgot, you didn't go to church much, did you? You broke your mama's heart." Boy, Po'thole was long on memory but short on forgiveness.

"Lucy Lu, Sheriff Munster has requested the honor of my presence in his office at ten or I'd go with you to the circle meeting." Gosh, I sure hoped God didn't strike me dead for lying about going to the circle meeting.

"Ha! He's arresting you for Bobby's murder." She was almost giddy with excitement. "Wait until I tell...."

And, whoosh, she was almost out the door before I caught hold of her shirt. Because of the heft and weight of her force on barreling through the door and my desperate attempt to keep her from spreading any rumors, the buttons on her shirt exploded and went rolling everywhere.

Lucy Lu was standing there, totally uncovered. Well, she did have on a Victoria's Secret bra and, I must admit, she filled hers out far better than I did mine.

I started to laugh, as did the counter girls, and the one other customer in the coffee shop. "I'm sorry, Lucy Lu. I'll buy you another shirt."

Antonio Buglia walked through the door. He is Po'thole's new police chief, formerly of New Jersey, and his nickname is, what else, Tony Bugs. It was bad enough that he was from New Jersey and with a nickname like Tony Bugs it was highly suspected in most circles around town that he might have had Mafia connections. In fact, Gracie Blanche had whispered to me during the Old

Fashion Antique and Art Show that the Mafia was interested in taking over Po'thole.

My comment was a simple, "Why?"

Apparently, I don't understand the massive appeal a small, rural farming community would have for the Mafia. Everyone else, well, according to Gracie Blanche anyway, believes Po'thole is just worth a boatload of money to the Mafia and what better way for the Mafia to gain inroads to this pot of gold than to send an Italian police chief down to take over the town.

Lucy Lu beyond horrified that a city official would see her precious naked body was screaming, "Don't look! Don't look!"

Tony Bugs, being the fine upstanding law officer that he was, grinned. "Why Lucy Lu, I do believe that's the Victoria Secret's Wonder Bra, isn't it?"

What happened next really wasn't pretty. Lucy Lu lunged at Chief of Police Tony Buglia. Although I thought Lucy Lu had given me the evil eye earlier, it was absolutely nothing in comparison to the look she was glaring down on Tony Buglia. She was actually foaming at the mouth.

"Don't look at me, you piece of New Jersey Mafia crap! Tony Bugs, you turn your back right now! You mobster you!"

I would have bet you even money that Tony Buglia knew his nickname was Tony Bugs. I was wrong.

His olive skin turned a deep fuchsia color. "What did you call me?" he roared. Stepping forward and catching both of Lucy Lu's ample wrists in his hands, he turned her around and slapped cuffs on her so fast that I felt compelled to applaud his performance. Apparently that was not the way to impress him.

"Who are you?"

I decided it would be a good time for me to exit. "Nobody. I'm just a nobody." I tried to scoot out the door. Unfortunately, Lucy Lu was still blocking the door. I surmised that while I wasn't much for attending church, she had never gone to Weight Watchers either.

Lucy Lu decided it was time to take me down with her. "She's Parker Bell and Dewitt is going to arrest her for the murder of Bobby Derlicter! She's meeting him at his office at ten."

"Lucy Lu, put your shirt back on." He had his hand on his gun and his eyes were piercing mine.

She wailed, "I can't! You have me in handcuffs!" She proceeded to cry.

Speaking loudly, Tony said, "Wanda Sue, come out from behind that counter and take my key..."

The counter girl rolled her eyes, "No. I ain't getting anywhere near criminals. My mama done raised me right." She immediately ducked beneath the counter, where upon you could hear the girl calling 911. "Yes, operator, there's a lady in handcuffs, a guy with a gun, and a crazy woman here. Help!"

Tony and I looked at each other like we were the only sane people in the coffee shop. I decided to take the initiative and spoke first, "Um, Chief, I'm just supposed to meet Dewitt in his office. It has absolutely nothing to do with Bobby's murder."

"Put your hands on your head and turn around."

Okay, now I was pissed. I still hadn't tasted my sip of coffee yet, the drama that was unfolding before me was suddenly not amusing, and so far I wasn't going to vote for anyone as Mr. or Ms. Congeniality. I had had enough of the shenanigans. To heck with a quiet vacation in Po'thole, to heck with Homeland Security, I was ready to go back to Atlanta.

"Call Dewitt. I'm on my way to his office." And with that I scooted past Lucy Lu and out the door.

Tony made absolutely no effort to stop me. Lucy Lu was screaming something at the top of her lungs at me but since I wasn't paying any attention I really don't know what she said. I'm assuming it wasn't anything that was encouraging and uplifting.

By the time I got to Dewitt's office, I was in a foul mood. My coffee was cold, it tasted like cardboard that had been soaked in hot water, and I had paid for something that was now undrinkable. I still wasn't awake, my new computer had not arrived yet, I desperately needed hot coffee, and I felt the beginnings of PMS starting. I wanted to hurt someone bad.

The redhead sitting behind the countertop with bulletproof glass barely looked up, "Sign in." What special kind of stupid person would walk into a county government building and try to shoot a receptionist? The criminal mind in a rural community must have a different kind of thought process than those living in the larger cities.

"I have an appointment with Dewitt."

She rang Dewitt's secretary and in about two seconds flat Dewitt was bouncing through the door. I swear it looked like he had had an infusion of life breathed into him. Apparently, the only time the man felt alive was in this building. I had never seen him so animated. It was scary.

"Parker, Parker, do come in!" Dewitt was making a big show to anyone paying attention. "Why, Parker, I do hear you had a little, shall we say, episode down at the coffee shop." He was grinning from ear to ear.

I was starting to feel really mean. I held my hand up. "Dewitt, before we go any further, I have to have a cup of hot coffee. I absolutely can't discuss anything without a cup of coffee. Where is your machine? I'll just help myself."

By this time, we had walked back into the inner sanctum of the building. Whoever decided on the gray-green colors of the Sheriff's Office building should be shot. There was nothing that felt good about the place. Dewitt waved at one of the many green uniformed women sitting behind desks. I guess he never realized that the green sheriff's office uniforms and the building walls matched so well that it looked like the wall was moving when a person walked around in the office.

"Gloria, get Parker a cup of coffee, will you?" She waited until Dewitt's back was turned and then rolled her eyes.

"Just black and *thank* you." At this point, I didn't care if Dewitt had the Pope on staff and had told His Holiness to get up off the throne and go get me a cup of coffee, at least I had good enough manners to say thank you. I have been known to just glare at someone until they brought me coffee.

Ever the gentleman, Dewitt stepped aside and let me enter his office first. The first thing I noticed, sitting behind Dewitt's desk and prominently displayed, was an autographed picture of Dewitt and Roger Moore, one of the many movie James Bonds. Roger was smiling and Dewitt had him at gunpoint in the classic James Bond pose. I was surprised. I thought Dewitt was more of a serious individual. He was a connect-the-dots type of person, point A leads to point B, and point B leads to point C.

His office was so filled with awards and plaques, framed letters of honor and appreciation I wondered when he had time to do any actual work. I also wondered how he had managed to acquire said awards and plaques.

He shut the door as I sat down in a tired-looking leather chair. "Parker, I understand you had a little, ah, situation this morning."

It was astounding how fast news traveled in a small town. It had taken all of five minutes to get from the coffee shop to the sheriff's department.

"Big D, please I really need a cup of coffee before I can give you details." I felt my head really starting to pound. Did the coffee manufacturers add nicotine to the caffeine so America was totally wired and addicted at the same time to a legal beverage? I couldn't go two hours without coffee or a soft drink. It was now going on three hours. I was a woman on the edge. I was well on my way to becoming dangerous.

Someone knocked on the door. "Sheriff Munster, I have the coffee."

"Bring it on in, Gloria."

Gloria had no idea how badly I needed that coffee. I was like a junkie looking for her next fix. I almost snatched it out of her hands.

"Gloria, thank you, thank you, thank you."

It was hot, it was black, and it was glorious. As the liquid made its way down my throat, I could feel my vision returning to normal, my pulse evening out, and my charming personality once again bubbling to the forefront.

Shaking my hair out, I could now face Dewitt and anything else the day might throw at me. "Okay, Dim...ah, Dewitt, what is it that I can do for you?"

His smile engulfed the entire room. "I understand that you had a little incident happen down at the coffee shop after I left. Tell me about it."

"Well," I paused, taking another big gulp of coffee. "Lucy Lu, you know her, right?"

He nodded and I gave him the short version of what had happened, concluding with, "Can I get another cup of coffee?"

Dewitt was laughing at this point, I was grinning, and, magically, another cup of the nectar of the gods had appeared. I was starting to enjoy my day.

"Who is that guy, Dewitt? I've only heard a little bit about him." The only thing I knew about Tony Bugs was what Joe D. had told me last night in bed. I really hadn't been paying attention.

"His real name is Antonio Buglia. Goes by Tony and his nickname is Tony Bugs. There's quite a few folks who think he's Mafia-related and he's trying to take over Po'thole."

"Is that really true?"

"Well, only time will tell on that. The truth is, or what I've been able to find out through my law enforcement contacts, is that he was police chief of a small town in New Jersey and is very quick to point the finger at others.

"Rumor is that he had political aspirations and backed the wrong group. He apparently was very vocal about his guy losing, saying the elections were rigged, etc. and here's the good part." Dewitt leaned forwarded conspiratorially. "He had a visit from an allegedly very connected man who strongly encouraged him to move south. When Tony had a visit several weeks later from that same gentleman, and the lovely weather in Florida was again mentioned, Tony kicked the guy out of his office.

"Two days later his police car blew up. . . just after he had gotten out of it. Tony didn't put the two together."

I started to laugh. "Dewitt, you mean to tell me Tony Bugs is dumber than anything I've heard around town?"

Dewitt nodded, smiled, and folded his hands behind his head. I was starting to appreciate Dewitt a little more.

"How did he get this job?"

"Turns out the former police chief Johnny Piesacki knew a guy who worked with Tony and told him the whole story. Johnny figured if he could get Tony Bugs down here Johnny could be hired as a consultant to the police department while maintaining his retirement money. Pretty slick, huh?"

"Well, a little double-dipping never hurt anyone."

"Anyway, he called New Jersey and told Tony Bugs what a soft, cushy job it was in Po'thole and he could spend most of his time fishing and having fun. Very little work to do, in other words. Tony thought about it for about three minutes and agreed.

"Well, the city commissioners are pretty much a bunch of patsies and whoever the chief of police tells you they want for a replacement, they go along with it.

"Tony gets down here and decides he doesn't want Johnny as a consultant. He wants one of his cronies from up north to be the consultant. Well, Johnny didn't take kindly to that suggestion and in the middle of a healthy discussion," Dewitt held up his fingers and made quote signs in the air, "Johnny falls over dead from a heart attack. It turns out Tony doesn't even know how to do CPR."

Dewitt shook his head sadly. "Can you imagine a police chief not knowing how to do CPR? Anyway, Johnny was already dead and they couldn't revive him and that, boys and girls, is how Tony Bugs got his job."

Wow! What a day this is turning out to be and we haven't even gotten to lunch yet. Who said small towns couldn't be fun?

"Who's running the department then?" I asked.

Dewitt's smile returned. "Probably his secretary, Erlene."

Erlene Thompson was older than dirt and had probably been with God when He formed the earth.

"Big D, um, is she still the same Erlene I remember?"

He nodded. "Yep, old, crabby, and you had best be a Baptist to get any good information out of her."

"How's she getting along with Tony Bugs then? What with him being a Yankee and all?"

"Rumor is that she keeps him occupied with paperwork, meetings, and speaking to various civic organizations while she basically runs things. Apparently that's what she's been doing for years. She certainly did it for Johnny when he was chief."

Oh, great! Po'thole has had a murder and the only one running things is a crabby old secretary without any formal police training. I sure hoped the national news media never picked up on that. Crooks, scam artists, and other undesirable rift raft would come pouring into town. Po'thole could potentially turn into crime heaven.

"So, Parker, are you going to write a book on Bobby's murder?" Dewitt was leaning forward, indicating a very high interest in my answer.

The alarm meter went off in my head. Something was up. There was a hidden agenda here somewhere and I wasn't sure I wanted to find out what it was.

"Um, not really, Dewitt. I mean, I know Bobby was a very successful businessman but I don't see that there would be any real national interest in this murder." I leaned back in my seat, took another sip of coffee, and joked, "Of course, if you have another couple of murders, then there might be something interesting to a national audience. Why, what's up?"

Dewitt was still smiling. "Well, Parker, I think it might be nice if you were very close to the investigation and had access to all of our information."

Alarm bells in my head turned into a Code Red Homeland Security Alert. I put down my coffee.

"You know it's an election year." He leaned back slightly in his chair, staring at me intently.

"Yeah, so?"

"Well, if there were a book being written about the murder and you had complete access to the sheriff and his investigation, don't you think...?"

BAM! The lights finally went on in my brain.

"Whoa, there, Dewitt! You are asking me to help you win your election by writing a book?" I just shook my head. "Just because I write a book, right now, today, the earliest it could be published and out in the bookstores is two years from now. Your election will be long over by then. What would the point be?"

He looked dejected. "Really? It takes that long to get a book out?"

I nodded.

He brightened up. "Still, it would be a feather in my cap to have you, a nationally known bestselling crime author, write a book on me."

No, no, no my brain screamed at me. I took a deep breath. "Dewitt, if there were a book involved, to be written, it would be on the murders, not on you personally."

"Why not?"

"Because no one cares about the sheriff. Readers only care about the murders and how they were solved, the interesting little details that were going on while the public was being fed other information.

"Readers would not be interested how you came up through the ranks, how you barely win elections, how you..."

BAM! Dewitt's hand slammed down on his desk. "Forget it, Parker! I can see you have no intention in promoting how good law enforcement protects the citizens of our county."

I stood up. His phone rang. We looked at each other for a long five seconds. He held up his finger for me to wait a minute.

"Yeah. What?" He groaned. "When? I'll be there in a minute."

He stood up.

"You might want to come with me. We have a three car fender bender." He fixed me with a hostile glare. "*That* might be of interest to you."

"Thanks for the coffee. I'll see you around."

"Thanks, Parker," his voice was dripping sarcasm, "I won't be needing your help."

As usual, he was wrong.

CHAPTER FOUR

Craziness

The aroma of fresh doughnuts wafted through the door every time it opened. Sleepy-eyed patrons sat at the various tables and booths in the small shop. Quiet murmurings floated through the air. Every so often the crinkling sound of newspaper pages was heard. I decided to try the doughnut shop after the disastrous day I had had yesterday at the coffee shop. Little did I know what was in store for me.

I was standing at the countertop talking to Penny Burton, the sweet little gal that owned the doughnut shop, when the Lady Gatorettes swarmed in looking not much different than they had in high school.

Myrtle Sue, Flo, Misty Dawn, Rhonda Jean, and Mary Jane, were five married hormonal women and had been friends since elementary school. They scared the holy be-jabbers out of me, and everyone else, back in high school. You just never knew what they might do. As adults they were even *more* scary.

Penny groaned. "Why me, Lord, why me?"

She explained the Lady Gatorettes met once a week for coffee, doughnuts, or anything else that put them on a caffeine and sugar high. They were borderline emotionally stable at best, but during their "special time of the month" they had a tendency to go a wee bit over the edge.

Their husbands practically begged them to go shopping, eat out, or do anything else that would keep them out of the house and away from them and the children. The men all wondered if they could receive severance pay from the government for post-traumatic stress disorder. Social Security was looking into that for them. Their wives, obviously, had no clue. Myrtle Sue's husband wanted to create a support group for the other husbands. But men being men, they didn't want to look weak and so the group never took shape.

Penny obviously dreaded their arrival. When she saw them coming in she dove for her emergency supply of Valium under her countertop. I, on the other hand, just wanted a cup of good coffee and to be able to drink it in peace and quiet. Apparently, that wasn't to be. *Maybe I should figure out how to use the ten coffee pots sitting at my house. Oh, wait! I've already burned the bottoms of two of them.*

From what I gathered, they were unusually quiet. Sitting at their favorite table, where Penny had placed their morning donuts and coffee, they just looked glumly at each other.

Penny would later say she should have realized a storm was brewing with them. They were never quiet when in the store. Between the caffeine rush and the sugar high, they were hormonal ticking time bombs. It was like listening to a bunch of chattering monkeys, she said.

"You know Parker Bell's back in town," flatly stated Myrtle Sue. She was eyeing her glazed doughnut crumb fingers like a cat focused on a helpless bird. The coffee shop table was littered with doughnut crumbs and empty cups of coffee.

"Hey," I offered, figuring if they were going to say anything nasty about me at least they'd know that I know.

They all looked over at me and then turned back to each other.

"Geez, Louise, girl, eat that doughnut! Stop picking at it!" Misty Dawn slammed her fist down on the table so hard that all of the doughnuts and coffee cups heaved up like a seven-point earthquake. "Myrtle Sue, I swear…"

"Which broom are you riding today, Misty Dawn, huh? You riding the 'I'm on my diet and nobody messes with me' or is it…"

Misty Dawn had the social graces of a jungle monkey. She reached across the table before any of the other Lady Gatorettes could reach her and squished Myrtle Sue's doughnut between her fingers.

"Um, good." She slurped her fingers, daring Myrtle Sue to retaliate.

Myrtle Sue gave her a look that was neither loving nor kind. "Go ahead, Miss Po'thole Witch, and eat my doughnut 'cas all of that fat is going right on your big old fat behind.

"In fact, your big old nasty butt is already hanging off that nasty broom and…"

Rhonda Jean murmured, "No, no, no." She put her coffee cup down. Coffee just did not make a lovely fashion statement with her Gator orange and blue ensemble.

Why, I wondered, couldn't I just get a decent cup of coffee with peace and quiet in Po'thole? I felt like I was watching a bad TV show.

As Misty Dawn started to push back in her chair, Rhonda Jean grabbed her arms and pulled them behind the chair. Mary Jane was opening the emergency Valium bottle she kept in her pocket, and Flo was holding a glass of water.

"Now, honey, you know this is the best thing for you." Flo spoke soft and slow.

Misty Dawn shouted obscenities and as she opened her mouth to curse at Myrtle Sue again, Mary Jane rammed a pill in her mouth and Flo put the glass of water up to her lips, tilted it and forced Misty Dawn to gulp it. It was the Lady Gatorettes' version of water boarding.

Myrtle Sue stuck her tongue out at Misty Dawn.

"Aarrgghh!" screamed Misty Dawn, pulling her arms forward with such speed and power that Rhonda Jean admitted later she thought God had bestowed unusual Samson-like physical strength on Misty Dawn. She thought it was a sign from God and released Misty Dawn's arms. After all, who was she to stand in God's way?

Myrtle Sue suddenly realized that her sugar-rushed, Valium-induced nemesis was probably going to kill her before the drug kicked in and dashed for the door.

Penny ran around from behind the glass doughnut case yelling, "That's it! You guys get out of here! This is the last time I'm putting up with you! Get out! Leave!"

Misty Dawn, distracted for only a moment, turned toward the slightly smaller Penny. Myrtle Sue rushed past me, frantically mashing her remote car key to unlock her car before Misty Dawn realized she had escaped. She jumped in it and barreled out of the parking lot.

"Dial 911 now!" shouted Penny over her shoulder while Misty Dawn was slinging tables and chairs out of the way. Good help being hard to come by in Po'thole, apparently none of the employees understood they were *actually* supposed to pick up the telephone and call for help. "Little Dwayne, pick up that phone and call 911 before I get hurt!"

Little Dwayne just stood there and watched. His mouth hung open. He didn't pick up the phone.

Penny screamed at him, "You idiot! Your fanny is fired! Someone, any of you, call 911 for help! Call the darn cops!"

Unfortunately, it never dawned on me to call 911 either. I was still drinking my coffee in the midst of World War Three. Joe D. *did* question my order of priorities when we discussed it all later.

Misty Dawn was still slinging things out of her way when she suddenly stopped. She sat down hard, looked up at Penny for a moment, and then flopped over on her side, snoring.

"Well, y'all, it did take a little longer than usual for her medication to kick in," drawled Flo, carefully picking up napkins and coffee cups.

"Out! Get out of here and never come back! I will file a restraining order against every one of you Lady Gatorettes!" Penny's anger caused little spittle flecks to foam at the corners of her mouth. "I have put up with you guys for years. Get out!"

Mary Jane, trying to act appropriately humbled, said, "Now, Penny, we'll help you clean up this mess. We'll…"

"You'll do nothing, missy! Out! I mean it—out!"

"Penny, you know Misty Dawn's been a little tense lately."

"Have you lost your ever-loving mind? The woman is wound up tighter than a Duncan yo-yo! She's been wound this tight since the day she popped out of her mama's belly. I have really had it with you guys. Customers are afraid to come in here because they could be hurt. I'm losing money on you. I want you out of here!"

Penny eyed each one of them. "Oh, yeah, before you go, give me $20 to clean up this mess and buy some more coffee mugs."

Flo looked at Mary Jane and Mary Jane looked at Rhonda Jean. "Pay her."

"Ah, how are we going to get Misty Dawn out to the car? She's out cold." Rhonda Jean was looking dubiously at the crumpled form on the floor. "You know she weighs a boatload. I can't lift her on my own."

Penny looked at them, shaking her head. "Little Dwayne, pick up Misty Dawn and take her out to the truck."

Little Dwayne shook his head as he was pulling off his apron, "Unt un, you done fired me, Miss Penny. I ain't doing anything."

Flo said, "Little Dwayne, there's five dollars in it for you, if you'll help us put Misty Dawn in Rhonda Jean's truck."

Cash bribes always work well in Po'thole and that's how Misty Dawn ended up in the truck. Well, she was put in the bed of the truck since they couldn't figure out a way to squeeze her in the cab. She continued to snore deeply and peacefully.

Rhonda Jean and Flo were in the truck, getting ready to drive Misty Dawn back to her house, when Mary Jane stuck her head through the open window.

"Look! There they are!" she screamed.

Those of us who were still in the doughnut shop had wandered out to watch Rhonda Jean and Flo maneuver Misty Dawn in the truck bed.

We all whipped our heads around in unison. Two brand new black SUVs drove past the doughnut shop and turned into the local convenience store.

"Darn furriners!" hissed Flo as they got in the truck and drove off.

I went back into the doughnut shop wondering what was going on.

"Say, Penny, what's the big deal about those SUVs over there?" I nodded towards the convenience store.

She snorted as she refilled my mug. "Well, rumor is them A-rabs are coming in here and buying up property in West River so they can start their own version of a South Mecca. They shouldn't be allowed to buy property if they aren't US citizens."

"That doesn't make any sense. Why would they be meeting up at the convenience store here if they're buying up property in West River?" My radar antenna had gone straight up in the air.

"Don't know, Parker." Penny was straightening up her store. "All I know is they show up a couple of times a week over there. They have New York license plates on them and they've bought property from some of the folks out there.

"And," she said as she nodded her head toward the parking lot. "That's part of the problem with the Lady Gatorettes. They've got their panties in an uproar about them A-rabs and the locals that are selling them property. They just don't think that's right. Them girls are upta no good."

About that time, Po'thole's finest pulled up in the parking lot. The police car's door opened and the officer was struggling to get out of the car. By the time he had gotten out and inside the store, Penny had a cup of coffee waiting on him.

Sweating profusely, he waddled over to the counter and eyed the mess in the store. "You pressing charges this time, Penny, or you just call me down here to look like you doing something?"

Penny sighed. "Yep, get the forms out."

The officer surveyed the damage, pulled out a notebook, and swiveled toward me.

"Parker, did you set those girls off?"

I swear, there must be a conspiracy in the universe because everywhere I go something weird happens.

"Yeah, of course, I did. I haven't seen them since high school. They became overwhelmed with my devastating good looks and went berserk knowing they and their pathetic little lives haven't changed one bit since high school while I, on the other hand, live an exciting life." With any luck, I wouldn't be arrested for obstruction of justice—or for being a smarty pants.

"If it wasn't Parker who set them off, what did?" The officer turned back around to Penny.

She was busy sweeping up the broken dishes and bits of half-eaten doughnuts. She just shrugged.

"Do they really need a reason? They're just crazy. Give me the forms and I'll fill them out later today. I'll bring them down to the station later this afternoon."

The officer drank his coffee, handed her the paperwork, then left and I was the only customer Penny had in the store.

"Penny, how long has this been going on? Who's selling their property to those Middle Eastern guys?"

She shook her head. "Lady Gatorettes? Since Christ was a child. Guess you can find out at the courthouse about the sales."

Looking at the clock and then back at me, she said, "Parker, I got to get ready for fixing lunch for the new security team out at the power plant. Catch ya later."

Whoa! A new security team at the power plant? What was that about? Homeland Security had called my Atlanta office requesting that I take a much needed vacation to Po'thole and do a little snooping around. Have to admit though, I still wasn't sure what they wanted me to look for. Homeland Security had their fingertips on every county in the United States and when property was sold to Middle Eastern-sounding names it triggered the real estate tax collector's office computers and that information was then forwarded to them. Racial profiling? Yes, of course, and it was always done under the guise of national security.

I had received the call from them asking that I come down to Po'thole and see if I could find out what was going on. Basically, I was being paid to listen to the local gossip and then report it back to Homeland Security. I figured it was easy money and not much work.

"Penny, what new security team is at the power plant?" I slapped a five down on the counter top.

Busy cleaning up the mess from the Lady Gatorettes, Penny answered over her shoulder. "They're guys out of some security company in Jacksonville and have been hired to protect the power plant."

She looked up. "From *what*, I don't know. Actually, they look like Navy Seals."

I cocked my head and raised an eyebrow. "What's going on with the power plant? Are they doing security for both plants?"

"Geez, Parker, I don't know. It's the Bigby plant. I don't know if they're doing anything at the Roscoe plant."

My mind was spinning with the possibilities. What were military people doing at the power plant and why a new security company handling everything?

"Penny, anything new being built at Bigby's?"

"Not that I know of. Come back later, Parker, and ask the guys. They're really friendly."

I thanked her, then went out to my car in the parking lot. The cold air conditioning felt great in the Florida heat and humidity. Looking for the number on speed dial, I pressed it, and was connected to my office.

"Missy."

"What's up, Parker? Need another laptop?"

"Nope, find out why there's a new security team at Bigby's, find out what is going on or being built there that requires a new security team, possibly military in nature, and find out if the same thing is happening at Roscoe's. Call me when you have something." I disconnected the call.

There was no point in calling Homeland Security—I didn't have anything to report and only a slight suspicion that whatever was going on with the A-rabs might be connected to the new security team at the power plant.

I headed on over to the convenience store. Okay, so I'm nosy. Sue me. I justify my nosiness as doing research for the government.

The black and gleaming SUVs had New York license tags. I walked into the store. It looked exactly like every other foreign-owned convenience place I had ever been in: somewhat dirty, an odor that defied definition, overpriced canned food, tons of munchies for those drug-induced food attacks, four kinds of cheap beer, tons of cigarettes, and prominently displayed on the countertop, Swisher Sweets. But no one else was in the store other than the blond-haired kid standing at the cash register.

Two brand new SUVs in the parking lot but no people in the store. What was going on?

I nodded at the kid. "What's up with all those SUVs and there's only me in the store?"

The kid nodded and smiled. I couldn't tell if he even understood English although he looked like a typical blond surfer kid.

"Do you speak English?"

He smiled.

"Do you have any Coors Light?"

No flash of recognition at the mention of my favorite beer. I knew he was the watch guard, but over *what*? I decided to push the envelope a little to see what was going on. I walked over to the cooler door and was just about to open it when a high-pitched, ear-piecing whistle sounded behind me. I half-turned to make sure it was the kid doing the whistling and not some maniac I hadn't noticed coming through the door.

Nothing. No one rushed out of the coolers, absolutely nothing. The kid was now going berserk whistling but nothing was happening. I turned back around, put on my winningest smile, held my hands up, and said, "Hey, buddy, it's okay. I'm just looking for my beer. Where is it?"

He was still whistling those shrill high-pitched sounds and he was making me very nervous. Me, being the brave soul I am, decided it was time for me to leave.

There was just more craziness in Po'thole than I could stand.

CHAPTER FIVE

Lady Gatorettes

As I drove home I started adding together bits and pieces of what I knew about the Lady Gatorettes.

They were faithful patrons of The Capt'n's Table, a dining and drinking establishment located on the St. Johns River. They had been known to run off the end of the dock into the murky but deliciously cold water to quench the fire of a hot flash. God help whoever was in their way when one of them started running. At least a road kill death was quick—a Lady Gatorette running over you meant broken bones and a concussion. Death to the unfortunate soul was probably not an option.

They were die-hard University of Florida football fans. In fact, obsessive was an understatement with these, ah, ladies. Not being fortunate enough to have the $14,000 or so to be in the Bull Gator Club, or even having enough money to get season tickets, they were nevertheless as supportive of Gator football as they could be by watching all of the games on TV. They knew every player and his statistics by heart.

I had heard they had pooled their grocery money together for one month and bought a big flat screen TV. Their husbands and children weren't exactly happy that they ate greens, beans, and cornbread with an occasional hot dog thrown in, for a month. The Lady Gatorettes didn't care; they had their big screen TV for football season.

The Lady Gatorettes had formed shortly after the girls had gotten out of high school. None of them ever thought about leaving Po'thole and so none of them aspired to further their education. They were very content to spend the rest of their lives where they'd grown up.

They formed the Lady Gatorettes to get back at Bobby Derlicter, who was the Gator Club president the year he had had the audacity to tell Rhonda Jean that the girls were not of the "social caliber" that the Gator Club wanted as members.

That irritated the girls to no end. So they decided to come up with their own predictions of how the Gators would do during football season. They took out a weekly ad in the newspaper with their predictions of the score. They were actually pretty darn good at it and the local sports editor did not make his predictions until after he had read the Lady Gatorettes scores. Even with him having advance knowledge of their predictions, they were almost always dead on with the exact score. It was scary.

It was heavily rumored that the Las Vegas bookies would call one of the girls at the beginning of each week to get their take on what the football score would be for that Saturday's particular game. If that was so, the Lady Gatorettes, had to be pretty stupid. Knowing the girls as I did from school, they would've either gotten a lot of money or they would've been out in Vegas partying all the time and I knew that none of them had ever been to Las Vegas.

To say that the Lady Gatorettes were an embarrassment to the officially sanctioned Gator Club was an understatement. As much of an embarrassment as they were to the club, Robert Joseph aka Bubba Joe Smith, the most current president, had decreed that they were to be totally ignored and anything that they might do would elicit no comment from them.

The bad news about the Lady Gatorettes, besides them being hormonal, was that they were basically good old girls who knew how to hunt, shoot, and track animals in the woods. Once, after consuming at least six beers, Myrtle Sue bragged that she had tracked her husband down during hunting season when he had "escaped,"— her words—from the house without asking her permission. Southern boys during hunting season don't believe it's necessary to ask their wives for permission to go hunting or explain why they go off in the woods with other men to get sweaty, nasty, dirty, and still don't have a dead animal to show for what they were doing over the weekend.

Apparently, it was that time of the month for Myrtle Sue and she had come home from a particularly bad time at Wal-Mart and discovered that her husband, the erstwhile J.W., had gone off for the weekend with the boys and left her a note saying he would see her Monday morning before he went to work. And, oh, yes, could he have clean clothes to wear on Monday?

Myrtle Sue saw red. She vowed that J.W. wouldn't have clean clothes for the remainder of hunting season because he'd made the fatal error of not saying, "I love you" on his note.

After becoming a graduate of the 90-day Myrtle Sue School of Doing Your Own Laundry, J.W. now leaves notes with a great big I Love You. Who says men can't be trained?

Although I had gone to school with the girls, we weren't what I'd call close personal friends. The Lady Gatorettes were good folks to cover your back although you didn't necessarily want to take them home to meet mama.

Flo is a tall, slim waitress with long blond hair who is now on her sixth husband and makes one mean strawberry pie. Flo's reason for having so many husbands was because not one of them appreciated and loved the Gators as much as she did. This did not make for a happy marriage as far as she was concerned.

"Humph," she sniffed. "If my husband doesn't have a clue as to who the quarterback is, what type of offense the Gators are running, and who the coaches are, then what good is he to me?"

Of course, none of the other girls could figure out how she could possibly marry a man without noticing he knew nothing about the Gators. They just guessed the old cliché of "love is blind" was true. Apparently, Flo was very blind when it came to men. She also only dated men when it was not football season and that probably explained why she never noticed why they knew nothing about football.

Myrtle Sue, a little dark-haired fireplug of a woman, is a domestic goddess. She surfs the Internet constantly looking for new information and statistics on the Gators. Her husband, while not understanding a single thing about the Gator football team and could care less, worships the ground his wife walks on and he is more than pleased as punch to accommodate her. As long as he gets at least one hot meal a day he's a happy camper. He has been known to brag that Myrtle Sue makes the best sandwiches that could be eaten with one hand while driving his tractor out in the potato and cabbage fields.

Mary Jane, a very attractive brunette way back when, went to Atlanta for a weekend with some out-of-town cousins upon graduating from high school and upon her return has never seemed quite right. There was much speculation that she had indulged in some cheap street pharmaceuticals and that was the reason why she's just never been quite right. No one knows for sure—she's never explained—and her out-of-town cousins disavow knowledge of anything. They also have never visited her ever again. And, she does get a nervous tick in her left eye any time someone mentions going to Atlanta. She has been known to mutter, "It's the devil's playground."

Apparently not realizing New York City is bigger than Atlanta and there's a lot more sin there, she moved there for a brief moment in time. She thought she was in love with the city that never sleeps at night, changed her mind after a year, and came back. She's still a redneck but now has an educated palate. She also dates guys that she meets on the Internet. While the rest of the Lady Gatorettes occasionally scold her for surfing for men on the Internet, they are all secretly envious of her.

Rhonda Jean is the trick play master. She knows every trick play that had been in a game for the past thirty-five years. She also annoys the heck out of the coaches at Florida because she creates and sends in new trick plays every week during spring practice and the regular season. Rhonda Jean's fervent wish is that one of her plays will be used during a televised game and the Gators will run it in for a touchdown. So far it hasn't happened.

Her husband, Big T, short for Thomas the Third, was pleased as a pig in mud and mighty proud of his wife every time she received a letter from the coaches. He just knew that one day one of his wife's plays would be used and then they would both be national celebrities. That's the reason why Big T gave up chewing for dipping. Dipping didn't turn your teeth as brown and he was very proud of his big smile. Also, he didn't want to look like a big old Southern redneck on national TV. The bad news is, Big T poached game and all the Fish & Game Commission people knew him all too well.

Misty Dawn, so named because that's what the morning looked like the day she was born and her mother took that as a naming sign, sent encouraging cards and notes to all of the football players who had played in each game. She was tickled pink when one of the players mentioned on national TV that it was her cards and letters that helped him during the difficult ordeal of his brother being arrested for dog fighting. His brother is still sitting in jail and, no, Misty Dawn, doesn't write him. She only writes to the players.

Misty Dawn, unfortunately, isn't quite as dainty as what her name might indicate. She has the vocabulary of a cross-country truck driver. And, oh, yes, she has a very short fuse on a very hot temper. The woman carries grudges like Christians forgive sins. The other members of the club were always trying to convince her that most of what happened around her was not a personal attack. It was people just being people.

It's too bad that Misty Dawn had not joined the Navy. Swift, silent, and deadly, she would've made a natural Navy Seal. The only person she never got mad at was her husband John Boy. She thought he walked on water.

John Boy worked construction and was afraid of no one; however, he absolutely quivered when she walked in the house with that death-to-the-world glint in her eye. Until she had vented all of her frustrations, he knew there was no reasoning with her.

The one time he had not let her vent, she had gone out to the chicken house and they ended up eating chicken for a month. He was just glad that the only thing she had killed was fifteen chickens. As he confided to J.W. one night over beer, he was mighty happy he didn't have pigs or cattle on his ranchette because Misty Dawn might've killed them, too.

When the Lady Gatorettes decided to do their version of a quasi-nude poster and sent it to the UF football department, that's when things got a wee bit out of hand. Somehow that poster ended up on YouTube with the fighting Gator song playing in the background.

The ladies thought it was great fun and they were beyond happy about being in a video on the Internet. As far as they were concerned, they had attained national celebrity status.

They convened later that same day at The Capt'n's Table. That started a rather enthusiastic discussion and called for more beer than they normally consumed. Many ideas were tossed out on how they were going to get on national TV and, of course, give their beloved Gators a "shout out."

These girls were scary enough without alcohol but once they started drinking there was no telling what their plotting and planning would lead to.

Fortunately or unfortunately, local reporter Butch Lane was at The Capt'n's Table that day and took copious notes of what happened next. He had shared the story with me over a couple of frosty frothy liquid libations one evening and we both agreed it would make a great book.

Misty Dawn, on her third draft beer, said, "We need to capitalize on our celebrity status. I would just love to see us on the Today Show."

"Don't you just know that would piss off Bobby and...?" Rhonda Jean lifted her Dr Pepper and they all laughed.

"I tell you I think we should email every Gator club in the universe and tell them what we've done and encourage them to buy our poster." Myrtle Sue was gleefully seeing vast quantities of money in her checking account.

Flo, always a little man-crazy, excitedly said, "Frat boys! Frat boys will buy our posters!"

Misty Dawn snorted, almost blowing beer bubbles out her nose. "Are you crazy, Flo? Frat boys don't want to see us." She emphasized her words slowly and carefully. "We could be their mothers."

"Well, yeah, I guess so. We don't want to put any wrong thoughts in their heads." Flo mourned for a moment or two.

Rhonda Jean was wondering why she had never taken up drinking beer with the Lady Gatorettes. Then she remembered she was the only one who had never had a DUI ticket. She attributed it to always drinking Dr Pepper.

"Hush, girls! Here comes that jerk Bobby and the rest of the Gator club," hissed

Mary Jane.

"We need to give them a shout out if for no other reason than to piss them off." Misty Dawn was ready to go to war with Bobby. She was still mad at him for saying they weren't of the right social caliber for the Gator club. The girl could hold a grudge.

"Yoo hoo, Bobby! Yoo hoo, Bobby!" Flo stood up and was getting progressively louder the nearer Bobby and the group came. She wanted to force them to acknowledge her.

Bobby and the club ignored the Lady Gatorettes until Misty Dawn screamed, "Hey, lard butt, don't you got no manners? Flo's talking to you!" She was up on her feet.

Flo, realizing things were getting out of hand, tried to grab Misty Dawn and sit her back down. Misty Dawn, already a little drunk and who already carried more than enough anger and resentment against the Gator club, was ready to explode. She was struggling to get to her feet while Flo, Myrtle Sue, Mary Jane, and Rhonda Jean were doing everything they could to keep her in one location, preferably her chair.

"And you call yourself the *Lady* Gatorettes," snorted Bobby.

Having a blond moment, one of the other female members chimed in with, "Ladies don't talk like that, only white trash does!"

Wasting a perfectly good pitcher of beer, Misty Dawn threw it at Bobby and the other club members. Total mayhem broke out complete with screams and the sounds of broken glass.

Misty Dawn, with an evil glint in her eye and a wicked smile, suddenly stopped, stood up straight, and screamed, "Power to the women! Hear that, Bobby? Power to the women!"

All of the Lady Gatorettes later agreed that Bobby had turned white as a sheet, apparently haunted by less-than-desirable high school memories.

He turned around to the other club members. "Who wants to be in this place with them, anyway?" He strode purposefully toward the exit. The other members, keeping a cautious eye on the Lady Gatorettes, eased out the door.

The Lady Gatorettes started to laugh.

"I am freaking gonna kill him one day," stated Misty Dawn, trying to flag down their waitress. "Hummpphh, for him to say we're not of the same social caliber that just burns my goat."

"It's fries my goat," timidly said Rhonda Jean. "I was the one he insulted. Face to face and in person, I'd like to add. It's really not *your* battle, girl."

"Well, that twit insults one of us, he insults all of us. I tell you, I'm gonna get that boy one day. Messing with my girls. Dipweed!"

With a fresh draft now firmly in hand, she raised it. "Go, Gators!" Various cheers and shouts could be heard around the bar. "Go, Gators!" "Gators rule!"

Flo, Myrtle Sue, Mary Jane, Rhonda Jean, and Misty Dawn looked at each other, eyeball to eyeball, and with an almost imperceptible nod in agreement, raised their mugs. No words were necessary; they all knew what was meant...they weren't finished with Bobby yet.

CHAPTER SIX

Buddy

Buddy Walker owned the most popular sandwich shop in Po'thole. Actually, it was his version of an Old World Delicatessen; however, the locals still called it a sandwich shop. He was well known for his incredibly large sandwiches at reasonable prices.

Buddy was very proud of his European-style deli. A couple of times a year he would go to the deli capitals of the U.S.—New York, Philadelphia, and New Orleans to visit various other delicatessens so he could see how he could improve his.

After each vacation he would come back with an even wider girth. The man could gain weight like nobody's business. He was a cross between a big old huggy teddy bear and a penguin. He waddled when he walked. He and Jenny Craig were not personal friends.

Opening the door to his deli, the most delicious aromas just this side of heaven made my mouth salivate. Nothing shouted "deli" like the aroma of olive oil, onions, and various sandwich meats wafting up my olfactory sensor. Sausages, cheeses, and sandwich meats were beautifully arranged behind a very large and well-lit display case. He also had a wide selection of imported cheeses, wine, and beer in addition to serving out-of-this-world sandwiches.

Since coming back to Po'thole I found myself eating at his establishment at least three times a week. The top button on my pants was getting very tight. No wonder the man was so big—his sandwiches were huge. And since "Sweating to the Oldies" wasn't my idea of fun, I figured I'd have to stop eating there so much. The good news about eating at Buddy's was that it was the best place in town to catch up on all of the local gossip.

Buddy, as always, was behind the counter taking orders and filling them all the while gabbing with the customers. I was truly amazed at his ability to multi-task so well.

"Hey, Buddy, what's new in town?" I yelled over the chaos.

He was Po'thole's answer to Google. He knew everything. The only trick to Buddy was that you had to ask the right question. If you didn't, the answer might not be anywhere close to what you were hoping for.

"Third time this week isn't it, Parker?" He laughed jovially. "You and my cash register must have a love affair going." He winked. "Joe D. knows about this?"

About that time Joe D. walked in and goosed me. That caused me to let out a whoop. Let it never be said that I couldn't be the life of the party. Also, let it never be said that there was a party going on at lunch time, either.

"What the...?" I screeched.

"Aw, honey, it's just me being a little playful." Joe D. grinned, leaned forward to kiss my cheek, while discretely trying to feel up my lower one. The man never stopped thinking about sex. Of course, I didn't either when I was around him. Joe D. had that effect.

He winked at Buddy. "What's going on in the murder investigation, Buddy? You know I can't pry anything out of Dewitt."

Buddy laughed, "That's cause he doesn't *know* what's going on in his own department."

Buddy nodded. "Tell me what you want and I'll bring it over personal to you."

I ordered the Round the World. It probably had half a pound of ham, turkey, roast beef, pork, and salami, then add the lettuce, tomato, onions, and pickles and you had a sandwich that could be used as a small boat anchor. If I had the sense God allegedly bestowed me with, I would have split one of those gigantic subs with Joe D. but, apparently, I wasn't in line the day the Big Man Upstairs handed out healthy dining sense.

Joe D. smiled and acknowledged several of the townspeople. He leaned over and whispered to me. "You know as cute as I think your butt is, you might want to think about eating a *half* a sub from time to time. Things have a way of expanding."

"Yeah," I retorted, "like the size of your belly. It wouldn't hurt you, either."

"Parker, that's mean!" He tried to look hurt but started laughing instead.

Buddy waddled over to the table with our sandwiches—even bigger than normal.

"You're kidding!" I gasped.

He grinned. "It's the Buddy Special and only Joe D. gets it. Well, of course, you, as his guest, get it, too."

My mouth was drooling because there was even more good stuff in that sandwich than what I had ordered.

Joe D. had already started inhaling the sub. Between chews he asked, "So what's going on that Dimwit doesn't know about?"

Buddy leaned over the table conspiratorially. "Some of the deputies think Bobby had women upta the camp."

"How's that?" Joe D. was still gobbling his sandwich like he had never seen food before.

"Well, first of all, the way Bobby was tied up. Guys don't tie rope with a little bow in it."

Joe D. almost choked on the remaining bite of his sandwich. "Say what? There was a bow in the rope? You can't make me believe that Bobby and the gang had a bunch of pansies up there!"

"See!" Buddy slapped Joe D. on the shoulder, "that's what I'm talking about! Those guys were only into women. Not even in their wild and crazy days would they have messed around with a bunch of pansies."

He paused and winked. "That means there must have been women up there."

I was now having to guard the remainder of my sub from Joe D.'s lecherous gaze. "That would have had to have been a pretty strong woman to kill Bobby and then put him on the spit roaster."

Buddy leaned back, wiped his hand across his sweaty forehead. "Yeah, I know, and that's where it bogs down. I don't know no woman who's that strong. Not even," he turned and pointed to the noisy group of women coming through the front door, "one of those Lady Gatorette women could do that and a couple of them are pretty strong."

"What did you say about us, Buddy Walker?" demanded Misty Dawn, walking over to the table. She had that beady-eye "let me start something now" look. She would have had made an excellent prison warden. But, of course, I was *never* going to suggest that to her.

"Um, hi, Misty Dawn." I was at least trying to be reasonably polite. The woman still scared me.

"Parker Bell, you stay outta this. It's between me," and she jerked her head toward Buddy, "and him. What evil, malicious thing did you say about me this time, you old fat..."

"Whoa, whoa, whoa, there Misty Dawn." Joe D. stood between Misty Dawn and Buddy. "If you're having a bad day, I'm more than happy to buy your lunch for you. Go on up to the counter and get what you want and I'll pay for it. But lay off Buddy. This was a private conversation and had absolutely *nothing* to do with you."

Joe D. looked down at Misty Dawn. She finally took her eyes off Buddy and looked up at Joe D.

"Who made you Mayor, huh?" she sneered.

"You want me to buy your lunch or not?" Joe D.'s tone was very mild but I knew he was seething on the inside. He absolutely hated the Lady Gatorettes. He thought they were all just one nut short of being in the squirrel house.

"I can buy my own lunch and the only reason why you're doing this is to impress Parker."

"Yep." Joe D. gave a short chuckle. "You're right, I'm trying to impress Parker." He turned to me. "Are you impressed yet?"

Oh, great, now I was back in the middle of this can of worms. Why, why, why had I ever agreed to come back to Po'thole? The whole rotten trip was turning out to be a disaster.

"Misty Dawn, I came here on vacation and, God knows, I don't want any trouble. Could we please just finish our lunch and visit with Buddy?"

Buddy was still just standing there. As big as he was, the man was an absolute wimp if anyone raised their voice to him. He was almost shaking because Misty Dawn had frightened him so badly.

The other Lady Gatorettes, Flo, Myrtle Sue, Rhonda Jean, and Mary Jane, had found a table and were trying their darnedest to get Misty Dawn over to the table. Buddy's deli was always loud but they had raised the decibel up to ungodly with their shrieking.

Misty Dawn, now apparently bored, ignored us and sauntered over to the waving girls.

Buddy looked at us, shaking and sweating even more profusely, and whispered, "I just wish they would never come in here. Joe D., you are paying for her lunch, right?"

Joe D. rolled his eyes and handed Buddy thirty dollars. "Whatever this will buy, okay?"

Far from being a romantic lunch, it had turned into a stressful meal. I needed an Alka-Seltzer. The Lady Gatorettes had that effect on my digestive system. But then they seemed to have that effect on every business owner I knew, too.

Joe D. and I returned to my abode, originally intending for a romantic afternoon. However, after eating a sandwich full of onions, olive oil, and garlic-infused deli meats, it didn't seem like the most appealing idea.

Joe, of course, did not agree with my assessment.

On the third slow, deep, sensuous kiss, I relented. My will power was squat with Joe D. I won't say it was exactly a romantic afternoon but it was full of action and laughs. And, sometimes, all you need is a fun afternoon.

About six, his cell phone started ringing. The ring tone was, "Please Release Me." How fitting for a certified public accountant to have that as his ring tone. Joe D. looked at the caller ID with a puzzled expression.

"Yeah," He answered. He nodded his head, looked over at me and rolled his eyes. Me being the astute person I am, decided to take a shower and leave him to his intriguing conversation.

I don't care what anyone thinks, I believe, yes, I believe *all* men think showers are sexy. I have never had a man not get into the shower with me, particularly if he thinks he might get some loving, which is always.

Joe D. squeezed in behind and wrapped his arms around my middle.

"I can't believe you're thinking of sex again when that's all we did all afternoon." Please note, I wasn't really complaining, I was just making a statement of fact.

"And your point would be what?" He nuzzled my neck while his hands were learning Braille over my body.

Okay, so we were in the shower until the hot water ran out. I hate cold water worse than Joe D. does. Besides which, we had, um, finished the shower.

"So, Parker, do you have anything to eat?"

I swear, men only think about sex and food.

"I'm single and I don't cook. Why would I have food? I think there's peanut butter in the kitchen cabinet."

Eating a peanut butter and jelly sandwich over the kitchen sink, he asked, "Want to know what that phone call was about?"

I cocked an eyebrow at him while chugging milk from the carton. I must have an extra male gene in my body somewhere that makes me do that.

"Buddy was found dead at the deli."

"Heart attack?" Frankly, that wouldn't have surprised me one bit as big and overweight as he was.

"Nope. Murdered."

I had just started on another chug of milk and this news caused the milk to explode from my lips and my nose, drenching Joe D. in the process.

"Say what?"

"Yeah, he was found just a while ago."

"How? What? Why?" I sputtered. I felt tears welling up.

Wiping his hands on his jeans, Joe D. motioned for me to come closer to him. He looked like a lost puppy dog. His eyes moistened up. I thought he needed a hug because of Buddy's death. Foolish me. He had that come hither look in his eyes, again.

I protested. "Now, wait a minute, Joe D., you just ate and I haven't. Besides, which, we just had sex...twice...this afternoon. How much more do you think I could do?" I paused as he started to play grab-my-fanny. "Come on, Joe D., we need to go to see what's going on.

"Besides, you just found out about Buddy being murdered. How can you possibly think about sex after that?" I didn't understand his thinking.

"I need to be close to someone to help me with this pain I'm feeling." Okay, he looked sincere when he said it and it sort of made sense.

"They'll call me later and you don't want to see Buddy's bloated, nasty, dead body, do you?"

Well, he did have a point and sex was a whole lot more fun than looking at dead people. No vote was necessary.

An hour later, after another shower, we hit the road. Arriving at the deli, there were four police cars parked out front. Sad to say, but if there had been a break-in or robbery in any other part of town, the sheriff's department would have to respond because Po'thole's entire police department was parked in front of the deli. Joe D. immediately went over to Police Chief Buggs. He nodded a couple of times and waved me over.

"Chief, have you met Parker Bell, my girlfriend?"

Noting that ownership and possession was established quickly between the two men, I wondered what this particular turf war was about. I suspected it had to do with some un-named female. I didn't care what Joe D. did when I wasn't around as long as I wasn't introduced to some long-lasting and contagious germs—then he would be dead meat—literally. I would absolutely kill him if I picked up any STD's, although it seemed rather inappropriate to bring up that thought process up at the moment especially since we were at a crime scene with a dead body.

Chief Buggs smiled, showing dimples. "I've read your books, Parker, perhaps you would be kind enough to autograph them for me." He looked back at Joe D. "Maybe over dinner while you're here in town."

Joe D. almost came unglued. He was taking slow deep breaths. A snake could not have done a better job of focusing on its prey. His beautiful brown puppy-dog eyes turned into the death slit stare of a predator stalking its next meal. Someone who did not know Joe D. would have never suspected he had turned from a soft cuddly teddy bear-type into the ninja I-want-to-kill-you-and-hide-your-body-where-it-never-will-be-found persona.

It was so much fun watching two male gladiators fighting over me. It was heady stuff. I could actually see myself turning into Ms. Popularity in Po'thole. Okay, it didn't have the same social status aspect as if one lived in Atlanta, DC, or any large city, but, hey, I'd take it.

Was this Tony Bugs the same guy I'd met arresting Lucy Lu? This guy was charming. The other one was a bit of a dipweed. Had he totally forgotten about meeting me? Because I was daydreaming I didn't notice they were both staring at me. "What?"

Clearing his throat, Joe D. growled, "Well?"

"Well, what?"

"Are you going to have dinner with Chief Buggs or not?"

Chief Buggs was standing there grinning like he had won the lottery. It was not a hoping-she'll-agree-to-go-to-dinner-with-me smile—it was the smile of a victor. He *knew* I was going to dinner with him.

Oh, well, a little jealousy wouldn't hurt Joe D. We only dated when I visited Po'thole and that was primarily because no one else ever asked me out. It's not like *he* ever came to Atlanta to see me.

I smiled at Joe D. and batted my eyes at Chief Buggs. Yes, I can do the girly things once in a while. "Yes, Chief, I would like to have dinner with you."

Joe D. snorted.

Totally ignoring Joe D., and still wearing a big smile, Chief Buggs asked, "Is tomorrow night good for you? I know this great place in St. Augustine. You'll love it."

Let's face it, there are only a handful of restaurants in Po'thole and none of them are particularly good. The other aspect is none of them have changed their menu in twenty years and you knew if it was Tuesday, it would be a meatloaf or fried catfish or shoe-leather steak special. Boring.

Knowing that I could totally be bought with a good meal, I said, "Yes, and St. Augustine sounds great."

Joe D. snorted again. "Ready to go?"

I handed Chief Buggs my business card and he handed me his. "Call me on my cell and we'll work out the details. By the way, what's your first name?"

"Tony."

Joe D. turned and stomped back to his car.

"Um, I need to go. He's my ride. Call me about the time for tomorrow."

Joe D. was fuming. I was surprised that smoke didn't come out of his ears.

"Oh, come on, Joe D., it's not like you don't flirt with every woman in Po'thole."

"Yeah, but I don't make dates with them in *front* of you."

Well, he had me on that one and I couldn't think of anything clever to say so we rode the rest of the way in silence.

"I'll cancel it, Joe D. Tony was a real jerk arresting Lucy Lu." I tried to scoot over to him but he shifted in the driver's seat.

"You might want to go on home, Parker. I don't feel like having you spend the night."

I found my cell phone and called Tony. "Hey, Tony, it's Parker Bell from a few minutes ago. I just looked at my calendar and realized I already had plans for tomorrow night so I need to cancel. Um, that's a nice offer but I'm not going to be able to do the night after either. But, I'll be happy to have coffee with you any time. Okay, see you around."

Turning to Joe D., I batted my eyes and said, "See? I cancelled with Tony. Do you feel better now?"

He just glared at me and then his cell phone rang.

"Joe D. here." He listened for a few minutes, grunted a couple of times, and then said, "You're kidding. Okay, bye."

I was never surprised at his phone calls. They always sounded cryptic and probably were, considering he was a CPA.

So much for me trying to juggle two men at one time. There was a reason why I'm single.

"Well, they found out how Bobby was killed."

CHAPTER SEVEN

Theories

Everyone had a theory on why Bobby and Buddy had been murdered. Of course, whoever was talking or giving their version of how or why they were murdered always knew someone in the Sheriff's Department who had given them privileged information.

This meant, of course, that the Sheriff's Department had more leaks in it than a shrimp net, however, what else could you expect in a small, sleepy Southern town?

Sheriff Munster was distressed. With his re-election, hopefully, coming up in only a few months, he did not want nor did he need any problems. The murders took away from his ability to campaign very much. It did, however, gave his opponent, Brock Bear, the opportunity to criticize the way the investigation was going, *ad nauseam*.

Brock wasn't what one would call the brightest bulb in the box but he was good-looking and took every opportunity he could to stand next to Dewitt. Dewitt wasn't a big man to begin with and he seemed to shrink when he stood next to Brock.

What was worse was the national news media had picked up on the story and Dewitt was ill-prepared to deal with very pointed questions from outsiders. He preferred to deal with his deputies on a one to one basis versus them hearing about things through the local newspaper or TV stations.

He tried to talk his secretary into becoming the public relations person to the news media but she wasn't remotely interested in being on TV. She did, however, encourage him to find someone who could speak without having a heavy Southern accent and someone who could at least use correct noun and verb tenses. She pointed out the news media always seemed to find the least educated Southerner to speak on behalf of everyone.

The only person he had in his department who he felt the media wouldn't chew up alive was Rob Jonesboro. Rob was 6'5", three-hundred pounds, a gym rat, and who had a Masters degree in English Literature. Not something one would normally assume that a deputy sheriff in a small town in northeast Florida would have. Rob had discovered he didn't like teaching and he found great amusement in quoting Henry David Thoreau and Ralph Waldo Emerson to people he arrested. He knew full well they didn't have a clue as to what he was saying so he took delight in explaining the quotes to them.

His greatest desire was not to have arrest any people and that more of the crime-ridden-area kids would stay in school and develop a love for learning. He believed that education was a way out of poverty and a way to living a longer life.

Apparently, some of his quotes had an effect on the kids. Rob spoke at numerous church functions and civic organizations whenever he was asked. His topic was always "How English Lit Decreases Crime."

Crime in his sector decreased markedly. He made fewer and fewer arrests. People in the poorer, socio-economically depressed areas, also known as the entire River County area, would flag his car down and request a Thoreau or Emerson quote that would apply to what was going on in their lives. Rob, being the gentle giant he was, was always happy to comply.

Dewitt figured if he used Rob as media spokesman he would look good, Po'thole would look good and Southerners in general would look good. In short, Dewitt didn't see a downside. There was one — Dewitt just didn't think far enough ahead. It would come back to bite him in the fanny...big time.

Rob poked his head in Dewitt's office. "You called?"

"Yep. I am now appointing you as media spokesman for this office. We're starting to get calls from the national media about Bobby and Buddy's murders. I want someone who can string a few sentences together and sound intelligent."

Rob said, "Dewitt, this is your election year. Don't you think it would be better if you did it? It might help to get you some more votes and all.

"After all, Thoreau said, 'Do not worry if you have built your castles in the air. They are where they should be. Now put the foundations under them.'"

Dewitt glared at him. "You know, I never understand half of what those quotes mean. You're always spouting them off. It will sound good on national TV."

"Dewitt, it means..."

"I don't care! You're the new media spokesman. Just deal with it." Dewitt glared at him some more. "Is there a reason why you are still in my office?"

"What lies behind us and what lies ahead of us are tiny matters compared to what lives within us."

"*Get out of here now, Rob!*" Dewitt roared.

Rob nodded and left. Being smarter than Dewitt, Rob recognized a golden opportunity when he saw one. His big dream was to move into the national media spotlight promoting English Lit as a way to help curb crime. After all, what better way to influence more people and keep them from crime than to have the politicians recognize education was the key?

His next move was to contact someone intimately familiar with the workings of the press. Not having enough money saved to hire a media consultant to assist him with wardrobe, camera angles, and microphone etiquette, he turned to the next best thing. Me.

Yep, because I had written several crime bestsellers, Rob rightly figured that I was the one person who could help him. The bad news was I had absolutely no clue this was his plan, especially since I didn't even *know* Rob.

Rob was resourceful though. He knew Joe D. and he knew Joe D. and I had history together. He immediately called Joe D.

"Where there is an observatory and a telescope, we expect that any eyes will see new worlds at once."

"Hey, hey, buddy, what's happening?" Joe D. was always happy to hear from the Sheriff's office. He handled a number of their tax returns. Unlike many of the deputies on the force, Joe D. understood what Rob was saying when he quoted Thoreau. "So, new worlds are opening up to you and you need to see something more clearly. What can I help you with?"

"You dating Parker since she's been back in town?"

Joe D. chuckled, "Yes, of course. That girl just can't stay away from me when she's here."

"Do you think she would help me in knowing how to deal with the national media?" He then quickly outlined what Dewitt had told him and what his plans were. "So do you think she might help me?"

Joe D. laughed. "Let me work my magic on her and I'll let you know later. In fact, why don't you drop by the Capt'n's Table around seven? I'll introduce you and you can tell her what's going on and ask her if she would be kind enough to help you out.

"Let me be up front with you, if she turns you down the first time, don't worry about it. I'll talk to her later, know what I mean?" They both laughed.

Bless Joe D.'s heart, he was always willing to help a friend out.

I was slightly surprised to receive a phone call from Joe D. requesting the honor of my presence at the Capt'n's Table. I thought we were going to get take-out and stay home.

"Well," he chuckled when I reminded him of that, "we can relax later. I just thought you might like to watch the sunset over the river. You know how beautiful it is."

"That's true. Okay, you want me to meet you there or do you want to come by and pick me up?"

"Babe." And I could hear that cute half-smile that made me weak in the knees.

"Okay, I'll meet you there."

"How about wearing that low-cut shirt I like?"

Apparently, his appetizer of choice wasn't necessarily gator tail bites.

"Sure. See you later."

Okay, I admit it. The man could float my boat like no other. If only I could get him out of Po'thole! I just didn't want to live in a town where people had absolutely no clue about culture. My idea of culture wasn't drawing color hopscotch blocks on the hot sidewalk.

Out of all the places in the world I've traveled, Po'thole, thanks to its location on the St. Johns River, definitely had the most spectacular sunsets I've ever seen. The sky turns a smoky red blazing its final energy over the tops of dark green pine trees. The sunset holds its majestic color and then suddenly it's dark. I always loved watching the final throes of the day ending in such splendor while sitting on the St. Johns sipping a cold frothy liquid libation with the man who could make my heart go pitty-patty just at the sound of his name.

I was totally relaxed when a gigantic man stopped by our table on the open deck at the Capt'n's Table. Honestly, I just figured he was a friend of Joe D.'s and really wasn't paying any attention to him. I was watching the blue herons and egrets fly off to settle in for the night and vaguely wondering if they slept in the trees or hid under a bush.

"Parker, this is my good friend, Rob," Joe D. said, pulling me out of my blissful place.

Call it whatever you want to, but when Joe D. refers to someone as his *good friend* it indicates all sorts of things. It usually indicates he has promised something to someone and it usually involves me in some capacity. Those were not words I wanted to hear coming out of Joe D.'s mouth.

"No."

"What do you mean no? I haven't said anything except to introduce you to my good friend, Rob."

"No. You or," I nodded at Rob, "he wants something from me. I'm here on vacation and it seems like I keep getting sucked into things not of my choosing. You know this is one of the two-hundred bazillion reasons why I left this place to begin with, don't you?

"It's like a darn whirlpool to Hades. You can't ever escape once you're here. Whatever it is, the answer is no."

"Babe."

"No. I don't care if you are giving me a million dollars, the answer is no, no, no." I stood up.

"Rob, was that your name? I'm sure you're a nice guy but I'm leaving. You and Joe D. figure out how to do whatever it is he promised you."

Joe D. winked at Rob, obviously thinking I hadn't noticed but I had.

"Parker, come on, sit down and finish your beer. We're just making conversation," Joe cajoled.

I was determined to escape. "No. I see Myrtle Sue inside and I'll get her to take me home."

"Good lord, she's with the Lady Gatorettes and they're crazier than loony tunes," burst out Rob. "You might not be safe with those girls."

I cocked an eye at him. "I went to high school with them. They won't hurt me."

Joe D. implored upon my good nature again. "Babe."

Okay, now I was getting annoyed. Having a couple of beers in me didn't help matters either. "Can you say more than one word or is that the limit of your vocabulary?"

He started to say something and I stopped him. "No, no, no. A thousand times no." I got up and stomped inside.

The Lady Gatorettes had been making a lot of noise, the standard whooping and hollering that goes on when they're drinking, until I walked through the door. It suddenly became very quiet and I was acutely aware that I was wearing a blouse that was showing off my girls.

Although they were glaring at me through an alcohol-infused daze, Misty Dawn snorted and said, "What do you *want*, Parker? You've got the only two single men in the county out there and you're walking away from them."

Oh, mercy. Just what I wanted, a bar fight with the nastiest gal in the county. Let me point out that after a couple of beers my thinking was not exactly clear. Being out on the deck with Joe D. and Rob sure seemed like a better place to be than with the Lady Gatorettes. You just never knew what they might do and the fact that I had gone to high school with them did not mean one thing. I was frantically trying to remember if I had been nice to them during high school. I didn't want to end up in the St. Johns River...at night...where there are *real* gators in the water.

I grinned, "I just came in to tell you that I had a little chat with Joe D. and he has very kindly offered to buy you ladies a round of drinks."

"What the freak do you want?" snarled Misty Dawn, chugging down the last of her beer.

"Well, since we all went to high school together and I'm back for a little while, I just thought you might like a round." I smiled broadly.

Misty Dawn grumbled. "I know you want something."

"Shut up and let's get that round before they change their minds." Myrtle Sue had her priorities straight as far as I was concerned.

"Nope, just being friendly." I hope I didn't sound too over the top. I wanted this bunch of crazy hormonal women on my side should the need ever arise.

Rhonda Jean chimed, "Misty Dawn, Parker was always nice to us in high school. Let's just drink the beer." And then being the only completely sober one in the group because she only drank Dr Pepper, she said coyly, "That does mean a pitcher for each of us, right?"

I did have a fleeting thought of what I was going to have to do to keep Joe D. appeased since I was spending his money but, hey, he and Rob wanted something from me. Even though I didn't know what it was, I figured whatever it was it was probably an even swap.

"Sure, of course, Rhonda Jean." I was still smiling.

"I want your pitcher, Rhonda Jean." Misty Dawn eyed her carefully, "You're not going to drink it anyway."

Flo, Mary Jane, and Myrtle Sue all chimed in at the same time. "We'll share it!"

Misty Dawn glared at them so hard I doubt her own mother would have loved that look.

I left and went back out on the deck. I figured they could squabble amongst themselves.

"All right, what is it you want?"

Rob and Joe D. looked at each other and smiled.

"Oh, yeah, I should mention that *you*," I looked right at Joe D., "just bought each of the Lady Gatorettes a pitcher of beer because you're such a nice guy." I smiled sweetly.

"Do what? Are you crazy? That's going to be at least fifty bucks." I did have the impression that he might not be happy with me. *Oh, well.*

Rob cleared his throat. "It's probably a small price to pay, Joe D., to have Parker on our side and give us her advice."

Joe D. looked down in his beer and didn't bother looking up.

"Rob, what is it you want?" I was trying to be polite. The waitress looked out the plate glass windows and I signaled for another round.

"Okay, so here's the thing, Parker. You know Dewitt is running for re-election again and it's probably gonna be another squeaker."

I nodded my head and took a sip of the delightfully cold beer. There's nothing like a cold beer after a long, hot day, even if it was my third one.

"Anyway, you already know Bobby and Buddy were murdered."

I nodded my head again, wondering if he was ever going to get to the point.

"Dewitt wants me to be the media person and you know how much I believe that English Literature can help curb crime. I want to be articulate, smart, and I want to move up in the world." He said all of this in a rush, turning a little pink.

I looked at him and nodded. "You want to know how to look and sound good on TV and on the radio, right? You don't want to be the standard, stupid, Southern redneck deputy."

He smiled hopefully. "Can you help me do that, Parker? I would really appreciate it. 'A truly good book teaches me better than to read it. I must soon lay it down, and commence living on its hint. What I began by reading, I must finish by acting.'"

"Thoreau?"

"Who else?"

"You do realize that most of the media isn't well-versed in brainy quotes and Thoreau, don't you? So, you'll come off really well by saying various quotes and, actually, if you have your statements typed up so you can hand them out to the reporters or have a website where they can download it would be good also. The easier you make their life, the nicer they'll be to you."

"What about, um, wardrobe, haircut, all that stuff?" Joe asked.

I looked over at him. "Do I look like a stylist to you? You're going to need some help in this area. Blue always looks good on TV but you're going to need some help."

I was thinking, never a good thing when I had had more than three beers, if I knew someone who could help Rob. I knew on a deputy sheriff's salary there was no way he could afford to have a couple of custom-made suits along with custom shirts. While I can be very generous, ask any of my employees, I wasn't inclined to adopt Rob.

Picking up my cell phone, I punched in a number, and heard the cheerful voice of my secretary Missy. "So did you destroy another laptop, Parker?" I heard a slight snicker in the background.

"Is that Denny behind you? Doesn't the man ever work? What does he actually do that I'm paying him for?" I grumbled. I heard a couple more snickers.

"Okay, where's Saffron these days?" Call me a coward, but direct dialing my book agent and getting her on the phone meant at least a thirty minute phone call and I really didn't want to talk to her after three beers. Plus, she would corral me into agreeing to write another book. Grudgingly I had to admit, she was an excellent agent and always managed to get me some super great advances. She was also a clothes horse and was always impeccably groomed. She would be perfect to help Rob and she might get him a book deal. I thought it was a win-win situation.

"Saffron? I think she's in Orlando at some type of convention. Do you need me to get her?"

I stood up and walked away from the guys. Quickly I explained what I wanted, closing with, "Just have her meet us in Jacksonville. Get me a day, time, and location. Do not, I repeat, do not have her call me under any circumstances. I want this to be a surprise for both of them."

Missy giggled. "You know she's going to call you directly and it will be from some number you don't recognize."

I snorted. "I'm only taking calls from numbers I know."

"Okay, if you say so."

I turned off my cell phone—that way if Saffron did call I wouldn't feel compelled to answer it.

"Gentlemen, problem solved." They hoisted fresh new cold mugs of beer to this announcement.

"I knew you could do it."

"Thanks, Parker, you're awesome."

"Okay, Rob, I have to know if you can get away from the office day after tomorrow for pretty much the whole day."

Rob focused his slightly glazed eyes at me. "No problem, that's my day off any way."

About that time, the bar door burst open, almost taking it completely off its hinges, and the Lady Gatorettes came running through the door squealing and stripping off their clothes as they aimed for the cold, dark, murky river. Let me hasten to say, it was not a pretty sight to see those women naked. The glare of pasty white skin—whiter than porcelain on a couple of the more Rubenesque women—was enough to blind a person, not to mention having to view some tattoos in areas better left for their husbands to see. I felt nauseous. Apparently, the guys felt the same way. We left the Capt'n's Table and headed over to Joe D.'s house.

The phone rang just as we entered the trash pit better known as Joe D.'s home. Shoving aside food wrappers from every fast food place in Po'thole, Joe D. found the phone. Winking at me, he said, "This is Joe D. How...um, yeah, sure, she's here. It's for you," he said as he thrust the phone at me.

"Hello?" I was trying to figure out who would know where I was when it dawned on me.

"Parker, darling, how ARE you? You know, I can get you a really nice advance on any new crime book you want to write." It was Saffron Woo, book agent extraordinaire, fashion diva, and the last person I ever wanted to talk when I had consumed god knows how many frothy liquid libations. I felt a headache coming on...and it wasn't from the beer.

"Saffron, did Missy tell you what I wanted?" I prayed, *Please, Lord Jesus, let this be a short phone call.*

"Yes, darling, she did. Wonderful girl. Meet me at 10 a.m. day after tomorrow at Barney Wong's. It's near Five Points. Bye. I have to go."

I didn't even have a chance to tell her what was going on. I looked dumbly at the phone, realizing that God does answer prayers and that we were going to get Rob some professional fashion sense. I vaguely wondered if I could write off this upcoming expenditure to my professional services budget. I could just hear my CPAs fussing. Oh, well, that's what they're paid for, to keep me out of trouble with the IRS.

Joe D. had already dozed off on the couch, surrounded by a really unhealthy amount of fast food wrappers.

Rob came out of the restroom. "Parker, um, if you're gonna spend the night here, you might want to be really careful when you go to, um, tidy up. That bathroom is beyond nasty.

"I hate to say anything ugly about Joe D. but, 'An unclean person is universally a slothful one.'"

"Thoreau had a quote for everything, didn't he?" I quipped.

"Yep."

"If you're trying to tell me that Joe D. is a pig, lives like one, and is somewhat lazy about cleaning his house, then, yes, I am fully aware of it. Meet us here, with coffee, at nine and we'll drive to Jacksonville."

Rob had no clue what he would be dealing with once Saffron Woo got hold of him. More important for me, I would get to watch her in action and not have to bear the brunt of her comments regarding my apparent lack of fashion sense.

She was definitely going to have to order a funeral suit for Rob the way people were being murdered in Po'thole.

CHAPTER EIGHT

No Patience

I had just spent a delightful evening with Joe D. It was actually one of our more romantic evenings. While CPAs aren't generally known for their romantic side, he had bought Ritz crackers and cheese whiz and put them on the nightstand. I could live with that.

Yes, even though I didn't live in Po'thole any more, I just couldn't bear the thought of selling my childhood home after my parents had died. I guess it was a way for me to remember the love in our household.

I must admit it did feel a little odd to have Joe D. next to me in their bedroom. Let me hasten to add, that it's the biggest bedroom in the house and, yes, I had purchased a new king-size bed before the room was ever christened with a male sleepover.

Phones ringing first thing in the morning are an annoyance and I recognized my Atlanta office's number on caller ID. That couldn't be a good thing.

"Why do you think Buddy was murdered?"

Probably an innocent question, except I was lying on my back and had just inhaled another Ritz cracker with cheese whiz. I choked, sputtered, saw stars floating in my eyes, and wondered briefly if CPR was going to be needed to revive me.

"What? How did you guys know about that?" *Mental note to self, check my clothes to see if there was an electronic bug planted on them.*

I could hear the grin in Missy's voice.

"Parker, Parker, Parker. Do you actually think we don't know what goes on in Po'thole when you're down there?"

Silence from my end; well, except for the grinding of my teeth, apparently encouraged her to continue her early morning harassment.

"Okay, here's the deal," she took a deep breath, "Sheriff Munster called our office trying to locate you, except that doesn't make any sense since you are already there in Po'thole, he knows that, he knows where you live, *and* he knows where Joe D. lives."

At this point I thought I heard a faint snicker in Missy's voice but since Joe D. was now nibbling on my neck, I couldn't be sure.

"And, if I'm not mistaken," she continued with a smug tone of voice, "he also has your cell phone number. Why is he calling us and why is he calling our office so early in the morning, Parker?"

Pushing Joe D. off of me, I scrambled to my feet looking for my jeans. I knew they were on the floor somewhere.

"Do you think he called because he's in trouble and he doesn't trust his own guys to come get him?" I was trying to think of any reason why Dimwit would be calling my Atlanta office over three-hundred miles away.

"Did you try to get a triangulation of where he might be?"

"Yes, Parker, and, um, this is pretty weird," she cleared her throat. "Um, ah, it's showing that he's right outside your house."

"Are you freaking kidding me?" I screeched. Monkeys within a hundred miles were probably trying to escape the sound. I was searching for my Victoria Secret push-up bra; my eyes were scanning the room searching for the bright pink lacy undergarment. Since we had stripped off our clothes in a frenzy, I knew it was somewhere in the room.

"Why? Where?" I was fuming.

"Parker, I don't know why but the where is a little, um, strange. It's right outside your bedroom window."

"I'll freaking kill him!"

By this time I had my jeans and tee shirt on. I put on my flip-flops and raced outdoors around to my bedroom window.

Nothing. Not a thing was there. No stomping on the azalea bushes, no footprints, no dead bodies, nothing. It looked normal.

"Babe, what's up?"

I turned to look at Joe D. who had followed me outside and told him what Missy had said. He looked around, scratched himself, and shrugged.

Missy was still on the phone. I was seriously irritated.

"There's nothing here. No one, nothing. What the fon-goo is going on?" I was totally perplexed. I looked like a bobble-headed dog whipping my head around.

"Parker, do we need to send someone down there to protect you?"

Missy wasn't joking. She was serious.

"Yeah, maybe. This is getting strange down here and it sure seems like I'm somehow connected to all of this."

"I'll send a rotating team of three. They will be there early afternoon." Missy clicked off.

"What's going on?" Joe D. grinned. "Shouldn't we finish this in the house?"

Men! Geez, do they all think about sex all the time? *Yeah, well, we all know the answer to that one!*

"Not now. Why is Dewitt's phone showing that he's here, right outside the bedroom window, and nothing's here? What the heck is going on? Nothing's been trampled; I don't see any signs of tampering with the window. In fact, it all looks normal." I was totally perplexed.

Joe D. seemed as befuddled as I was.

Standing back from the house, I scratched my head and looked around for anything that looked out of place. I knew my next door neighbors, the Weebles, were basically worthless when it came to hearing anything because, even though they wore state-of-the-art hearing aids, they couldn't hear a thing unless they were looking at it and even then that was debatable. Chances of them hearing anything was slim and none and they had both gone to the Bahamas.

Nevertheless, I decided to go over and ask if they had heard or seen anything out of the ordinary. I wasn't expecting much.

Knocking loudly on their door, I thought it must be hard to become older and watch the things you once could do become difficult or impossible to do.

A wavering old man's voice filtered through the door.

"Who's there?"

"It's Parker from next door, Bill. Could I ask you a question?"

Slowly—it seemed like an eternity—the front door opened. The little frail old man peered out hesitantly.

"How you doing today, Parker? Come on in."

He was agonizingly slow in backing up and turning his walker around. The man moved slower than a turtle in heat. I tried to think how I would feel if I were in his position. It didn't work. I just wanted him to hurry up so I could ask him my question.

"How you liking your new satellite TV?"

My mouth dropped open.

"What did you say, Bill?"

"You need to get one of these sonic boom hearing aids, Parker. They're great."

"Yeah, okay. What did you mean about the satellite TV?"

"These hearing aids are much better than the old ones I had. Why I can..."

"Bill, what did you say about the satellite TV?" I was starting to get exasperated. I hate to admit it but I don't have a lot of patience. I try, I really do, but let's just say, it's not one of my many natural gifts.

"Maybe I should get another one too...as backup. Do they give you a better price if your neighbor gets one too?"

"Bill." My voice was now starting to creep up into the shrill monkey range again. Not a good sign. Taking deep breaths to slow and calm myself, I tried again, speaking very slowly.

"Bill, what did you say about my getting satellite TV?"

"Huh? Oh, yeah. Those guys that came yesterday morning and installed your new satellite TV."

Since I hadn't ordered satellite TV, I wasn't sure what was going on. I went over to the window and looked at my roof. I didn't see anything.

"Bill, are you sure it was satellite TV people at my house yesterday? I don't see a satellite on the roof."

He chuckled. "Well, I saw people up on your roof so I went over there and asked what they were doing. They said they were installing a remote satellite TV."

Bells and whistles were going off in my head. My main concern was now that mine and Joe D.'s lovemaking was being broadcast on some amateur porn website. I felt nauseous.

"What remote satellite TV? Where did they put it?"

"On the roof."

It was like talking to a smarty pants three year-old child. Unfortunately, he had both Alzheimer's and Parkinson's in addition to his natural inclination to talk in circles. Frustration was usually the result of our conversations.

"Where on the roof, Bill? I don't see anything."

He waved his hand dismissively at me.

"What, Bill? Where did they put the remote?" I must confess I was almost shouting at him at this point.

"This too shall pass, Parker."

Gritting my teeth, I managed to eke out, "What shall pass?"

He grinned, waving his hands around.

"All of this."

I could feel smoke coming out of my ears and the top of my head. My eyes were turning red, and if I had been inclined to physically hurt someone, that would have been the moment. I shut my eyes, breathed deep, and counted to ten. I could have probably counted to a thousand and it would have made the same difference which was none.

"Bill, let me try again." I spoke very slowly in a loud voice. "WHERE ON THE ROOF WAS THE REMOTE SATELLITE TV PUT?"

He looked offended. "Parker, you don't have to shout at me. I have these new sonic boom hearing aids and I can hear you just fine."

I wanted to kill him.

"Bill, thanks for your help. I gotta go."

Clenching and unclenching my fists as I got out of his house as fast as possible helping my mental state somewhat. Seeing Joe D. back away from me as I approached my house, I realized I probably looked crazier than Bill Weeble.

"Apparently someone or possibly several people came over yesterday morning and installed a remote satellite TV."

Joe D. was looking at the roof line also.

"I don't see anything that remotely looks like a dish."

"Yeah, me either. I'm now concerned that we're going to be on some porn site after our activities last night."

He thumped his chest and grinned.

I came closer to the house, stood in the bushes and peered up. Sure enough, there was a small black cell phone taped to the edge of the eve of the roof.

A few minutes later I had it in my hand. It was an older version of a flip phone, small and compact. I cautiously opened it. Between the flip cover and the phone itself was a note. The note read, "Took you long enough! Ha, ha!"

To say I was irritated was a major understatement. I dialed 911 from my personal phone.

"911. What's your emergency?"

I felt like saying, "Since I've come back to this god-forsaken town, everything in my life has gone to heck in a hand basket. I want my life back!"

Instead I said, "Hey, it's Parker Bell. Dewitt's cell phone was duct taped to the roof of my house. Is he safe?"

"One moment, please." There was a long pause with those annoying periodic beeps to let you know the call was being taped.

"Sergeant Duckworth."

"Sergeant Duckworth, this is Parker Bell and I just found Dewitt's cell phone taped to the roof of my house. I'm calling to see if he is safe."

"At this time, the sheriff's office can neither deny nor confirm Sheriff Munster's presence."

"Danny, it's Parker here, not the freaking newspaper. What's going on? There are an awful lot of strange things happening."

"Parker, you are a writer, ergo you are the press, ergo, I'm not telling you anything."

Taking a deep breath and wondering why I even cared what was happening to Dewitt, I said through clenched teeth, "Okay, then, you are not getting the cell phone so you can check for prints and an electronic bug. You have a really good day." I slammed the phone down.

"What's going on, Parker?" Joe asked.

I filled him in. "You know, I don't have to stay here. I'm thinking I may just go back home. Sure you don't want to move to Atlanta with me?"

Those brown eyes just rolled up and he shook his head no.

"Let me make a couple of phone calls and see if I can find out anything." His eyes narrowed slightly. "Um, you can't be in here when I make them."

I stomped out of the house. I was angry and mad.

Killing off some of the local Po'thole citizens and kidnapping the sheriff sure didn't indicate anything meaningful to me. I couldn't figure out any real connection from them to me. Plus, I truly didn't think the murders and the kidnapping of Dewitt had anything to do with me. I just thought it was a weird set of coincidences.

Joe D. came outside as I was stomping the bejesus out of an already-dead azalea bush. Thank goodness no one from the Beautification Committee saw me doing this. They believed with all of their hearts that the azalea bush was in the Garden of Eden and was, therefore, sanctified. Seeing me stomp on a dead plant on my property was still enough to have me arrested for destruction of a dog-ugly bush that only looked good for two weeks out of the entire year. How they could have me arrested and on what charges I didn't know but I sure wasn't willing to find out.

I was still fuming when Joe D. said, "I think I might know what happened to Dewitt."

"What?" I managed to snort out. "And don't tell me he was kidnapped. I, we, already know that."

"Apparently, he was found out in the woods tied to a tree. Um, naked, and with the words 'ha, ha' spray painted on him."

"What's going on, Joe D.? This whole thing just keeps getting weirder and weirder."

"Doll, I have absolutely no clue. Although, I'm pretty sure whoever did this to Dewitt could have killed him if they wanted to. I'm kinda thinking it might be a warning to him. You know, like back off on investigating the murders."

I nodded. "I'm guessing he probably had a small winky-dink and the ha ha was about that."

Joe D. kind of grinned. "I hate to break it to you, honey, but guys don't look at other guys, um, winky-dinks. That's a girl thing."

That's when it dawned on me.

"Where are the Lady Gatorettes, Joe D.?"

CHAPTER NINE

Death Threats

I hate the sound of the phone ringing first thing in the morning, especially if it's before I've had my first cup of coffee. As far as I am concerned, *anything* before my first cup of coffee in the morning is one of the deadly sins in life.

Unless, of course, I have a warm, drop-dead gorgeous body in my bed. Okay, so I couldn't resist Joe D.'s advances. He was warm, snuggly, smelled terrific, and a wonderful kisser—what more could a girl ask for?

Joe D. snuggled up spoon style. "You going to get that?"

I extracted my arm and picked up the phone. I didn't have a chance to say a word. "Parker, Parker, Parker! Girl, you're sitting on a huge story down there and you didn't even bother to call me to tell me that this could make a wonderful new bestseller for you! Why didn't you tell me this the other day?" I silently groaned and wondered what had possessed me to even pick up the phone to begin with.

"Yeah, well, good morning to you too, Saffron." She claims to be first-generation American of Chinese immigrants. I have it on good authority that her real name is Delilah Brooke and she's from Greenville, South Carolina. She may also be Jewish.

All I know is she's made me an exorbitant amount of money on my last two books. I love her; I just don't love her first thing in the morning, especially since Joe D. was starting to let his hands roam.

"Parker, honey, I had to find out about these two murders on national TV. Can you imagine how my little ears picked up when I heard there were two murders in that tiny little town you're from in less than a week? Apparently, Po'thole leads the country in having no murders for the past three years." Barely pausing for breath, she continued, "Don't you think this warrants a book proposal? I'm pretty darn sure I could get this sold fairly quickly and get you another big advance. What do you say, Honey?"

It was kind of hard to focus. Joe D. was now nuzzling my neck. His soft warm breath and the fact that he was pressing his body hard against my back was causing me to care less about making money and more about, well, you know. A girl doesn't have to spell out everything, right?

Apparently, I must've been thinking a wee bit too long because the next sound I heard was a very loud and harsh, "Parker!"

"Yeah, yeah, I, uh, heard you. Actually, Saffron, I hadn't given it any thought yet."

"Parker," Saffron's voice softened with little tinges of delight, "you have a guy there, don't you?"

Busted. Rats!

"Um, let's talk when I see you, Saffron. I'll think about it. Talk to you later. Bye." I rolled over and looked Joe D. in the eye. "Did you have something in mind?"

We finally rolled out of bed about an hour later. Joe D. hopped in the shower while I was trying to find some coffee and maybe a Twinkie. Heck, I eat out most of the time when I'm not supposedly on vacation and, I should be ashamed to say it but I'm not, there are seldom any leftovers to bring home. I have what's called a healthy appetite. I was desperately searching the cabinets for freeze-dried coffee when Joe D. came into the kitchen and put his arms around me.

He nuzzled my ear. "Can't find any coffee, can you? That's okay, we can go down to the Golden Corral and get something. My treat."

Yeah, it had better be his treat. After all, he had sampled *my* treats.

"Well, I have some freeze-dried coffee and hot tap water. That will at least get us started."

He eyed me like he had just glimpsed what Hades might look like. "You're kidding, right?" He shook his head. "I now know why you go out for coffee all the time. You do know that there is something called a Keurig, don't you? It makes one cup at a time. It's incredibly easy and the coffee tastes great."

"It costs too much."

Joe D. laughed. "Oh, says you who spends three dollars or more on one cup of coffee."

Opening the front door, I wondered why I even bothered to take a shower when the outside humidity was approaching 200%. Another hot, humid day in the land of paradise. As I was grousing to myself, that's when I noticed a note on the windshield of my car. I knew it was not a love note from Joe D. because he was standing right next to me and there would've been no point for him to leave a note on my car. He spotted it at almost the same time I did.

"Un, oh, what's this?" He gently pulled it out from underneath the windshield blade. "Sweetheart, I don't think someone wants you to win Miss Popularity this week."

Snatching it out of his hands, I quickly scanned the note noticing that it was hand written.

"Ah, are you dating anyone at the moment who might wish me bodily harm that I should know about?"

I was going to be pretty pissed if he was going with someone and had not bothered to tell me. The normal health hazards aside—she, *whoever* that might be, seemed to want me dead. I was just so much safer in Atlanta.

Joe D. leaned over and kissed me. "No, babe, just you. You broke my heart once and I've never let anybody else in." He kissed me again.

"You are such a liar," I snapped. "You've been married three times." *Men!*

"I'm talking about someone you might be dating who is a lot more serious about it than you are."

He smiled and shook his head no. I had a sneaking idea that he probably wasn't telling me the whole truth, well, at least, about dating someone else.

A few minutes later we were driving to DeWitt's office to give him the note. I, of course, was starting to feel the effects of no coffee in my system. I should have just put the freeze-dried coffee in the microwave but then I remembered I had accidently set the microwave on fire the first morning I was back in town. Who knew that if all of the coffee bubbled up out of the plastic coffee mug that the mug would melt, sparks would fly, and smoke would pour out of the microwave? I hadn't gone to the big box store to get another microwave.

It wasn't going to be a pretty morning regardless of how great Joe D. was last night and this morning if I didn't get some coffee pretty soon.

Joe D. was happy. He was humming to himself. "Babe."

"Yeah."

"I know you live on coffee first thing in the morning. Why don't you have a coffee maker? Why are you offering me freeze-dried coffee and tap water? That's just plain nasty."

"I have ten coffee makers, thank you very much. I haven't been to the grocery store to get any ground coffee. It just seemed so much easier to get it out. And, with so many *wonderful* dining establishments here, I couldn't see any sense in grocery shopping."

As wonderful as Joe D. is, he doesn't always get the finer points of my sarcasm.

"Really? In Po'thole? Come on, Babe. As much of a caffeine addict as you are, I would think that you would have pots of coffee on at all times."

"I wish you wouldn't call me that. I am not your baby."

He rolled his eyes. "I would have thought with all of that wonderful loving we did you would be in a better frame of mind."

That pushed the last nice button in my brain. Grinding my teeth, I managed to ease the words out of my mouth. "I want coffee now. Find me a place to get some coffee."

"In there." We had arrived at the sheriff's office.

Dewitt's secretary at least had the good grace not to roll her eyes at me when I asked her for a cup of coffee. Dewitt came bouncing out of his office as soon as he heard my voice. He nodded his head.

We showed him the note and his only comment was, "Who do you think left this, Parker?"

Joe D. asked, "So, what do you think she should do?"

I, for one, wasn't overly thrilled that two men were deciding what I should do. Apparently, just the mere fact of my being female must have caused some weird ozone layer to dissipate so that the two men standing in my presence felt compelled to make a decision for me. I was starting to get steamed.

The only reason why I agreed to bring the note over to Dewitt was to see if it would aid him in his ongoing investigation of the murders. Heck, there might be some connection and now that Saffron had put the idea of a new book in my head, I wanted to be part of the *crew*, so to speak.

My brain was beginning to come back to life as the warm, delicious, pitifully weak coffee eased down my throat. Apparently there is some sort of physiological connection between coffee in my throat and my brain kicking into gear.

"Dewitt," I paused. "Obviously, there's a connection between what's going on and my being here. I have absolutely no clue as to how I fit into any of this but why else would I be getting strange notes on my windshield? Also, what's up with the Lady Gatorettes? I saw them the other night at The Capt'n's Table and it was real funny they were laughing and joking and carrying on until I got up to walk past them and all of a sudden they got real quiet and watched me walk to the ladies room. That is so unlike them not to be loud and boisterous all the time."

Joe D. said, "They're always loud and creating trouble. That's because they're drunk or on a sugar high all the time."

The man had absolutely no clue about women and hormones. It was no wonder that he was still single. Of course, Dewitt is boring as all get out, so that may have some bearing on why there was no wonderful little woman in his life either.

"Big D, I've known these women since we were in school. When they're loud, there's nothing to whatever is going on..."

Dewitt interrupted me, "Really? So all of those calls I get to come break up fights and their tearing up the coffee shop and other stores means nothing, right? At least, according to you, right?"

"That's all harmless stuff and you know it. It's only when they are quiet that they are plotting something big."

Joe D. grinned and looked at Dewitt. "Yeah, like that time they took your patrol car and put it on that island thing they made in the middle of that little retention pond."

I started to laugh. Visions of Dewitt's patrol car sitting on a tiny little patch of dry dirt and surrounded by water, was too funny.

Dewitt, back to his humorless self, snarled, "That wasn't funny then and it's not funny now."

"By the way, Dewitt, how did they get your car out there? Weren't you out in that area on some call?" Joe D. knew how to egg things on; I'll give the man credit where credit is due.

"We think they picked up the car and walked it over to the dirt." Dewitt's right eye had started to twitch.

"Oh, come on, Dewitt, those five women picked up your patrol car, waded through water three to four feet deep, held it up in the air for the twelve or so feet over there, and then plopped it down on that tiny little spit of dry land? You gotta be kidding me!"

The only one in the room not laughing at that point was Dewitt. Even his secretary who had come in quietly with more coffee, bless her heart, was trying very hard not to laugh out loud. I'm betting that wasn't the first or even the 30th time she had heard the story.

"Let's get back to the note you brought in," snarled Dewitt. "That other subject is closed."

"How *did* you get your patrol car back running the roads again?" I was still laughing.

Joe D. answered. "He called someone with a ditch hoe and they filled in one side of the retention pond."

"Folks, let's talk about this note." He turned around to me.

"Parker, how often do you receive death threats?"

"Since I've been back in Po'thole? Never."

"What I mean is do you have anyone who might have tracked you here and wants to do you bodily harm?" Dewitt was starting to get exasperated with me.

"Nope. Never. Keep in mind, the people I write about in my books are dead people and, generally speaking, they aren't inclined to leave me death threats."

Dewitt pushed a button on his telephone while looking from the note to me, then Joe D. "John, come in here a moment. Bring your kit with you.

"We'll get John to see if he can pick up anything off the note."

Bless Joe D.'s heart, and all of the rest of him, when he said, "Ah, by the time you get any prints, run them, and get the results Parker could be dead. Doesn't it take several days to get the results?"

"What do you propose for me to do?" snapped Dewitt. "If you want twenty-four-hour surveillance, then you do it. You're her boyfriend."

It's so cute watching two grown men battle over me.

"Gentlemen, you might not have noticed it but I don't live here anymore and, in fact, I have been able to take care of myself pretty well for the past however-many years."

About that time, my cell phone went off. "Excuse me, gentlemen." I turned my back to the two squabbling men.

"Yes, this is Parker."

"Parker, it's Missy. I'm calling to confirm you received your new computer." She snickered. If she wasn't so darn good at what she did, which is basically keeping me straight, I would have fired her a long time ago. As it was, she was worth her weight in gold.

"Yes, Missy, I have it."

"Saffron called here first thing this morning."

"Yeah, speaking of that, how did she know I was in Po'thole and how did she get the phone number? She didn't call my cell phone, mind you, she called the actual house number. You didn't happen to give it to her, did you?"

"Parker, I am insulted! Why on earth would I give your book agent, who's made you a ton of money—let me point that out—why would I give her your home phone number in Po'thole? I don't even have that number."

"Um, since you set up that phone down here in this God-forsaken place, I'm thinking that Saffron called and you gave her my number because you thought it might be funny. Would I be right on that?"

"What's going on down there, Parker? Do you need any help, any backup?"

While I considered her question, I thought about Missy's notion of Florida which was different from mine. Sure, there are palm trees and beautiful beaches. There's also more poverty, illness and hopelessness than in any other state in the union.

Missy got my attention. "Parker, Parker, are you okay down there? I think I need to come down there and help you out."

"No, Missy. I appreciate that but it's not necessary. I need you to stay there and take care of the office. Besides which, I thought you had said you were sending someone down here yesterday. Where are they? What else is going on?"

She brought me up to speed on a couple of things, I told her who to delegate them to, and then she dropped a bombshell on me.

"I was waiting to see if you really did need any help down there. I think you do. Denny is on his way."

"Denny is on his way where?"

"There."

"Here."

"Yes."

"Why?" I was confused. All I had done was request another computer. This did not warrant my former FBI man coming to Po'thole.

"He just said you needed help and he was driving down there."

"When did he leave?"

"Yesterday."

"Missy, why didn't you call me yesterday and tell me that? You apparently have no problem giving out my personal home number to Saffron but you can't be bothered to tell me that Denny's on his way down here? Geez, Louise, girl, what is wrong with you?" I was starting to work up into a good snit.

"How much is he going to charge this time? I'm sure you must have some sort of clue or do you care to share that with me?" I snapped.

I heard a long, slow deep breath.

"Parker, he said he was coming down there to help you and to check out whether he might want to retire there." She added helpfully, "He said the fishing was supposed to be good in Po'thole. It says so on the Chamber of Commerce's website."

My eyes started to cross.

"So, does that mean he's *not* to going to charge us on this?" As generous as I could be, I also keep my eye on my company's expenses. *After all, no one loves my company more than I do.*

"Well," she began doubtfully, "he didn't say anything about it."

I snorted. "Did you think to ask him? Nooooo, you did *not* because you did not think about it—it's not your job and it's not your company." I paused, I was getting ready to blow, and I must admit my slightly sarcastic side came out. "Or did you?"

"I'll call him right now, Parker, and I'll get back to you." She hung up before I could say another word, probably a good thing because I was getting ready to fire her.

In all fairness, let me point out, that I fire Missy a couple of times a year. It's almost like a ritual we have. In truth, I would trust Missy to cover my back with her computer keyboard any time.

Joe D. cleared his throat. "You okay over there, Miss Computer Expert, or do you think you could tear yourself away from your cell phone for a moment?"

My attention was quickly drawn back to the problem at hand. A note threatening my impending demise was not one I could assume came from an admiring potential suitor. Therefore, I could safely assume, he was serious about harming me.

"Okay, gentlemen, let's look at the facts," I went into my alpha female state. "We know whoever left the note on my car had to do that sometime between 5 and 7 a.m. Why? If it had been before 5 a.m., the dew on the windshield would have made the paper too damp to read since it was written with a ballpoint pen. As it is, the writing is a little blurred because of the dampness.

"If it had been done after 7 a.m., the ink wouldn't have blurred at all." I paused to slurp down some more coffee.

"Whoever wrote this wanted to be sure that I saw it first thing when I came out of the house. From a psychological standpoint, they wanted me to know they had invaded the sanctity of my home and property. It's more of a teaser type thing to put it on my windshield."

I looked at them. "The words 'you die' indicate they are very familiar with me, where I live, and what I'm doing. In short, whoever it is knows me and feels like they know me pretty well.

"What's interesting to me is what they think I know that's worth killing me for. Any ideas?"

"No." Joe D. could be the soul of brevity.

"Do they know you are working on Bobby's case with me?" asked Dewitt anxiously.

I rolled my eyes. "Dewitt, I am here on vacation. I am not working on a case. Apparently, I am the only person in Po'thole who believes that." I was exasperated. I had really only come back to help Gracie Blanche with the antique sale and help Homeland Security out.

Gloria poked her head in the door. "Dewitt, the Lady Gatorettes are tearing up the doughnut shop. We need to send someone over there."

CHAPTER TEN

Not-so-happy Jack

I stumbled into the coffee shop with a serious need for strong coffee. *That freeze-dried instant stuff really shouldn't be called coffee.*

"Coffee, black."

"Sure, Parker. Anything else?"

I noticed Penny wasn't her normally chirpy self.

"What's up, Penny?" I almost dreaded the answer. "Did the Lady Gatorettes do something to you?"

Shaking her head no, she said, "Happy Jack is dead."

"Happy Jack who?"

Soulful eyes looked at me. "You know, Happy Jack Canaday—everyone's friend."

The blank stare must have done it for her.

"You know, the car salesman. Happy Jack Canaday Used Car Sales."

"What happened?" I now had my coffee and could start to focus on life again.

"He was found dead at his desk early this morning. Dewitt was at the front door waiting for me to open and told me he was on the way to the crime scene. The only thing he knew at that point was Happy Jack was dead and he was flopped down in a sliced pork barbeque dinner."

I spewed my coffee out. "What?!"

"Yeah, he was a really nice guy. Came in here once a week and bought three dozen assorted doughnuts and a couple cartons of black coffee with cream and sugar on the side.

"You know what he did with the leftovers? He gave them to the homeless guys that showed up around three o'clock. He wanted to make sure they had something to eat that day." A tear slid down Penny's cheek.

I barely heard what she said. What did barbeque dinners have to do with Bobby, Buddy, and now Jack being murdered? That was the only common thread that I could see.

"Penny, is Happy Jack's in or out of the city limits?"

She blinked. "I don't know. I guess he might be outside. I wonder who's going to take over his used car lot."

By this time I had Dewitt's cell phone number on speed dial. I pushed my coffee cup back to Penny for a re-fill.

"What do you want, Parker? I'm in the middle of a crime scene investigation."

"Dewitt, are the barbeque dinners that the only thing all of these murders have in common or is there something else you're not letting out?" I paused, hoping Dewitt would take the bait.

A long pause, then a sigh. "Parker, you are not in law enforcement. You are a citizen, a citizen who is on a need-to-know basis."

"Dewitt," I mustered up all the charm I could without choking on my coffee at the same time. "I am also a best-selling author."

I could just see Dewitt's ears perking up, the radar swinging around in circles on his head, and visions of his picture on the cover of a best-selling book.

"Are you saying you're now going to be working on a book about these murders, Parker?"

Praying that my book agent Saffron Woo would make good on her promise to find a publisher, I shut my eyes, inhaled deeply, and said, "Yes."

"Okay, come on out. Oh, yeah, bring me some coffee and doughnuts for my guys."

Inhaling the sugary smell of the doughnuts and the aroma of freshly brewed coffee, I was in heaven as I put them on the front seat of my car. I turned the key. Nothing except for two small clicks.

I walked back into the doughnut shop. I yelled, "Penny."

She came out of the back room, wiping her powdery hands on her apron.

"What's up, Parker? Did you inhale all of those doughnuts?" she snickered.

"I...."

KABOOM!

Parts of my car shot through the plate glass window and zipped over our heads as Penny and I hit the floor. She screamed and I was pissed because my new cup of coffee was in that car.

I cautiously lifted my head to see what was left of my car when another *BOOM* rocked the doughnut shop.

I heard voices in the far recesses of my mind but I couldn't seem to move my body. My eyes wouldn't open and I drifted back into unconsciousness.

"Babe, can you hear me?" I heard the gentleness in Joe D.'s voice.

I groaned, tried to open my eyelids, but I couldn't.

"What?" I mumbled.

"She's awake. Come see about her." I guessed Joe D. was talking into some type of intercom. My brain was very slow and I couldn't seem to think clearly.

"What's happened?" My eyes still wouldn't open.

"Babe, it's me. The nurse is on her way in here. Your head's wrapped because you got hit right under the eyebrows by your GPS and radar detector. Um, your nose is broken too."

I didn't remember seeing anything before I passed out.

"Penny?" I croaked out.

"She's got a broken arm from where the hood of your car came sailing through the window. She put her arm up to protect her head."

"I'm gonna kill whoever freaking blew up my darn car."

Joe D. chuckled. "That's my girl."

Let me be really upfront about this: I am not a good sick person. I don't want anyone near me. If I need you, I'll call you but, otherwise, I just want to be left alone.

The nurse came bustling in the room. I could hear her and Joe D. talking in whispered tones.

"Hey!" I croaked out. "When are these bandages coming off? And I want to go home."

"Hey, Parker, it's Cindi from high school." Of course, why would it *not* be someone from high school?

Clenching my teeth and enunciating each word as carefully as I could, I said, "When. Are. These. Bandages. Coming. Off? I. Want. To. Go. Home."

"Parker, there are eight stitches on your eyebrow bone on the right eye. The left eye, same area, has nine stitches. Your nose is broken right between your eyes. In short, both eyes are swollen shut, and they are going to be swollen shut for several more days. You also have a mild concussion."

"Aren't you the one for cheerful news?" I sneered.

Ignoring me, Cindi continued in that polished nurse's voice. "I'm taking the bandages off later today but because you live alone, you need to stay here for a couple of days so we can keep an eye on you to make sure everything is healing like it's supposed to. Also, we need to be sure that are no complications."

I ignored everything else she said after that. When it was quiet, I reached up to pull the bandages off and found Joe D.'s hands wrapped around my wrists.

"Nunt uh. Babe, you can't do that yet. I do have some info for you though."

"Call my office and tell Missy…"

"She's already called me trying to track you down. Denny's on his way and should be here in a couple of hours. She said to tell you that the Arabs are buying up all of the lake property facing east. The only common denominator is the realtor."

My mind was reeling. Jack Canaday was murdered, my car was blown up, I was in the hospital, Penny had a broken arm, and the Arabs were buying up property like crazy around lakes. What was going on? What, if any, common thread connected everything? Were the Arabs just simply fascinated with building their own little oases? West River County was the last place on earth that would be welcoming to any outsiders, let alone those from the Middle East. Even the sheriff's department was cautious about dispatching officers out there, and most of them were good ol' boys. Did one person hate me, my car, the Arabs, and all of the dead guys? And if so, why?

The locals were anti-government to the nth degree, hated anyone who sounded even slightly different from them, and had been known to shoot at the Sheriff's cars for just fun.

"Joe D., none of this is making any sense. I don't know anything. Why would someone blow up my car? Plus, when would they have had the opportunity to set it up? I mean, I was in the doughnut store and I never saw anyone approach my car." I wailed, "I just don't get it."

Joe D. hugged my neck gently and kissed me on the cheek. "Babe, I don't know what's going on but I'll make some phone calls."

I drifted off into a comfortable, drug-induced never-never land.

*****

Cathy Jean Rogero, the realtor handling all of the Arabs' real estate purchases in West River County, was mentally counting her commissions and realizing she could be top realtor of the year in her office. She wanted to win the all-expenses paid 4-night, 5-day trip for two to Las Vegas. She had a new boyfriend and wanted to impress him. Vegas was only about two things: sex and shows. It was Disneyland for adults.

Her cell phone chirped. She grinned and thought *cha-ching*.

"Good morning, Amir. How are you today?"

"We have property around three lakes now. I want a total of six lakes and I want it finished in two weeks."

It was all Cathy Jean could do not to cheer. "I don't think that will be a problem. What's the ceiling price you want to spend?"

"What? I don't understand what a ceiling price is."

"Sorry. How much do you want to spend total on all of the properties?"

"Give each owner twenty percent more than what the appraised value shows on the tax records. All cash deals, close in two weeks."

"Amir, some folks might not be able to move out within two weeks. They...."

"Cathy Jean, you could be getting commissions from me and from them when they buy a new home. You are getting double commission. Make it happen. Make them happy."

"Amir, how about putting them up at the Holiday Inn Express in town for two weeks. That's going to be cheaper for you than having them try to up the price. Plus, I'll call Holiday Inn and get a discount. How's that?"

"Do it, make it happen. I'll call you at the end of the week."

Cathy Jean looked at her cell phone. Pure bliss and excitement was etched all over her face. Pushing down her greed to keep all of the real estate commissions to herself, she marched into her broker's office.

"Hey, David, it's great to be alive." She had on her winningest smile.

David, an old hand at real estate deals and reading his sales agents, chuckled internally at the brashness and drive of his heretofore barely-productive agent. What a few sales under someone's belt could do for their self-esteem and self-worth.

"Morning, Cathy Jean. What can I do for you?" He leaned back in his Executive 2000 leather and chrome chair.

"David, you know the A-rab guy I'm working with? Amir? Well, he just called me and wants to buy up property around three more lakes and he wants it done in two weeks." She paused, furrowing her perfectly shaped eyebrows. "I can't do it all myself so I wanted to get some of the other agents involved."

David grinned; these agents were so easy to read. "I feel a 'but' coming on."

She smiled, "But I don't want to split my commission in half with them."

After a few minutes of negotiation, Cathy Jean left David's office knowing she was still getting the bulk of her commissions.

The private line rang in David's office.

"Yep."

"Hey, buddy, what's going on?"

David chuckled. "Cathy Jean's guy just called and wants to buy up property around three more lakes out there in the west end."

"Really? That makes what, six lakes total?"

"Yes."

"Any clue as to what he's doing with those properties?"

"Nope. They're all cash deals and he's closing on all of those properties in two weeks."

"Wow! How much has he spent so far?"

"Probably not as much as you think." David laughed. "He's only spent about 1.5 so far and it should probably be about that same amount for the rest. So, give or take, about three mil for everything."

"What's he going to do with it?"

David laughed, "Don't know, don't care. It's good for everyone. He's paying twenty percent more than the appraised tax value of the property, he's putting people up at the Holiday Inn for two weeks, we're listing and selling the properties, plus selling the current property owners new homes, and I'm making money hand over fist. I'm happier than a cardinal in a warm birdbath."

"Where's he getting his money, David?"

"Don't really know and...don't care." they both said in unison, laughing.

"Have you checked this guy out to see if he's for real?"

"Yep, I have 2.5 mil sitting in my escrow account at the moment. As I understand it, he gave the Holiday Inn a black American Express to pay for everything."

"Whew! He's got some big bucks behind him then. A black American Express card? Wow!

"Hey, is this guy operating under his name or a corporate name?"

David cleared his throat. "That's confidential information, Joe D."

"Aw, come on, David, it's just me."

David squirmed. "If it were just you, it wouldn't be a big deal. But Parker's in town and is thinking of writing a book on these murders. You're hooked up with her—again—and I don't know what type of pillow talk you guys do.

"So, no, I *can't* tell you. It's confidential information."

******

Joe D. tapped his pencil on his lips in contemplation. This was some serious business. Because the properties hadn't closed yet, nothing was going to be on the tax rolls as to who had purchased the properties.

Dialing another number, he hoped he could get more information.

"Hello, this is Cathy Jean, River County's number one realtor. How can I help list or sell your property today?"

"Hey, Cathy Jean, great lead-in on your phone calls. It's Joe D. Savannah and I wanted...."

"Sorry, Joe D., I cannot answer any questions you have about anything pertaining to West River County." Her tone was formal and firm. "David just called me and reminded me of the realtor code of ethics. No info. Anything else I can do for you today?"

"No." He slammed the phone down. Tapping his fingers on his desk, he wondered who else might have some information. If the Arabs were going to develop the property, they would need to have a construction company.

Dialing Rodney Jones Construction Company's number, he hoped that call would reel in some more information.

"Rodney Jones Construction."

"Hey, it's Joe D. Is Rodney around?"

"One moment."

He doodled on his note pad for a few minutes until Rodney answered. "Yo, what's up, Joe D.?"

"Hey, I hear there's some Middle Eastern guys buying property out there where you are and I know they need that land cleared. I thought they mighta talked to you."

Rodney's voice was cautious. "Maybe. I talk to a lot of folks."

"So, if they did talk to you, what's their company name?"

"Joe D., whatcha fishing for?"

"Rodney, I just want to know who they are." Joe D. coughed. "What's their name or their corporate name?"

"Joe D., that's confidential information. I can't let you have that."

"Rodney!" Joe D. calmed his voice. "Rodney, you are a construction company. There's no big confidentiality ethics thing going on here."

"Joe D., you might not be aware of this, but my client base is confidential and I ain't sharing that with no one. You go be nosey somewhere's else."

Hearing the click, Joe D. was more curious than ever. Normally, he could get David, Cathy Jean, or Rodney to give him information. Of course, he shared information with them too. Nothing that would get him into any real trouble with the governing bodies of Certified Public Accountants, just stuff that might get him a hand-slap.

"Rodney Jones Construction."

"Hey, it's Joe D. again. Let me talk to Rodney." He was put on hold.

"Yeah."

"Rodney, how much are you being paid not to say anything?" Joe D. held his breath.

Click.

Joe D. called back for the third time. *Follow the money trail—that's always the way to find out what's going on.*

"Rodney Jones Construction."

"It's Joe D. again. Tell Rodney I know the answer."

"Mr. Savannah, Mr. Jones said to tell you not to call here again or he will file harassment charges against you. He also said to tell you he's sure it wouldn't be a good thing for your business if people knew you shared their confidential financial information with others."

Click. Joe D.'s mind was racing. He had obviously hit a major nerve with Rodney. For Rodney to threaten him with spreading malicious rumors in Po'thole meant that there was serious cash and/or threats on the line for him. He wondered what else was going on and how it all tied in with Parker.

******

Cathy Jean's phone rang. She was happy because with each ring of her cell phone it meant money in the bank for her.

"Hello, this is Cathy Jean, River County's number one realtor. How can I help list or sell your property today?"

A muffled voice. "Is this Cathy Jean the real estate lady?"

Smiling, she said, "Yes, it is. How can I help you today?"

"Stop selling property to them furriners or you're going to be a dead woman."

"Whaa..."

The phone went dead.

Tears rolled down Cathy Jean's face. Hands shaking, she called David. "Someone just called me and told me I was a dead woman if I kept selling real estate to Amir." She wailed, "All I'm doing is my job, David."

"Cathy Jean, come back to the office right now. And, for god's sake, be careful."

******

David was shaken. No one had ever threatened to kill one of his agents before.

Picking up the phone, he called the Sheriff's Office. When they answered, he asked to speak with Dewitt, immediately.

"Dewitt, here."

"You're not going to believe this." David proceeded to tell him everything that had transpired that morning.

David listened to Dewitt's reassurances that everything was going to just fine. He knew that Dewitt was stumped.

******

Hanging up the phone, Dewitt rocked back and forth in his padded chair. He needed to rattle a few cages. He found the number on a scratch piece of paper on his desk and called it.

"Hello?" A weary voice answered.

"Your boyfriend is in a world of hurt. Do you know what he's up to?"

CHAPTER ELEVEN

Put on Ice

I was stunned. Fighting through a haze of medications, I tried to focus on the voice.

"What? Who is this?"

"Parker, it's Dewitt, and Joe D. is skating on the edge of things. What do you know?" He took a deep breath. "Let me remind you, withholding evidence or knowledge of a crime or details of a crime to law enforcement is not a good thing. You could be charged as an accessory."

"Dewitt, I don't know what you're talking about." My brain raced furiously. What did Joe D. know or do that I didn't know about? *Did he have anything to do with my car being bombed?*

"Parker, he's making phone calls to people and threatening them. I've just had someone call in about a death threat." Pausing, he continued, "I'm asking you again, what do you know about this?"

Taking a deep breath, I said, "Dewitt, truly I have absolutely no clue as to what he's doing. We've both wondered, as I am sure you have too, who is it that's buying up all that land out in West River. I'm guessing he was making phone calls trying to find out who it is."

"Parker," Dewitt cleared his throat, "this is official now. If Joe D. is involved in any more threats or intimidation tactics, I will arrest him. Pass that along to him, will you?"

"Wait a minute," I was indignant. "If you are that all fired-up about him, you call him and tell him that yourself. I'm not your go-fer. I'm still laying in the hospital with injuries from my car being blown up. Got anything on *that*, Dewitt?"

I disconnected the call in a fit. *What is going on?* I never was overly fond of Po'thole or River County; hence the reason why I lived in Atlanta, but the place was more of a loony bin than I remembered.

The nurse came in about that time.

"How are you today, Parker?"

"When can I go home?" I snarled.

"When you have someone there who can take care of you. Probably another couple of days. Then you'll be released."

Taking a deep breath, I asked, "Would you dial a number for me on my cell phone?"

"Sure."

The phone rang twice and was picked up.

"Parker, what's wrong?" I had called Missy on her cell phone, and the only time I ever did that was when it was a serious matter.

"Get me out of here now." My voice was low and flat.

"Denny should be there by now. He's going to take you home."

"He's not. Get. Me. Out. Of. Here. Now." I was growling.

"What about Joe D., Parker?"

Much as I hated to say it, I wasn't sure about Joe D. at the moment. "Compromised."

A new male voice entered the room. "She's been signed out and she's going with me."

Denny, what a relief. Regardless of anything else, I knew Denny was trustworthy and had my back at all times.

The nurse was fussing and threatening to call security.

"Parker, I'm here. I've signed the paperwork and you're going home now. Is that Missy on the phone?"

"Yes." I croaked.

He took the phone from my hand. "I'm here. I'm taking her home now, and I'll call you when it's secure."

The nurse was still fussing as Denny lifted me out of the bed and put me in a wheelchair. Denny was an imposing figure. Ex-FBI, ex-black ops, he stood about six three and weighed in the neighborhood of two-hundred and thirty-five pounds.

"Your house is secure, Parker. Doc Naismith is with me and he'll take care of everything."

Relief flooded through my body. Not only was I sprung from the hospital but Denny would keep me safe, and Doc Naismith, a disbarred doctor who was also on several different corporations hush payrolls, would get me fixed up in a jiffy so I could find out why someone was trying to kill me.

Although the hospital wasn't happy about me leaving, Doc Naismith had waived around his beautifully-forged doctor's license and copped the, "I am God and you are not" attitude. The hospital, ever vigilant about the potential for a lawsuit and bad press, decided since I wasn't going to win the star patient of the year award, it would be best for all concerned to release me.

I was out of the hospital, in Denny's car, and home in less than forty-five minutes. Po'thole's a small town and the hospital is less than ten minutes from the family homestead. To say I was happy would be an understatement.

Although I still had the bandages wrapped around my head, my sense of smell had heightened considerably. The delicious aroma of freshly brewed coffee greeted my olfactory senses as I entered through the front door.

Almost giddy with delight, I shouted, "Coffee!" My hands carefully wrapped around a warm cup of the nectar of the gods.

"Ahhh! It's from Penny, isn't it?" I was slurping it down as fast as the temperature of the coffee allowed. The stuff they served in the hospital tasted like instant coffee with hot tap water. I could get that at home. It was *not* coffee.

"More!"

Denny laughed. "See, Doc? I told you, good coffee is the magic cure for everything with Parker."

My cell phone rang. I ignored it. It stopped, rang again, I ignored it.

"Doc, can you take these bandages off?" While the gift of sight is one that I truly treasure, I was determined to see today. Even if it wasn't much.

Unwrapping the bandages, Doc Naismith said, "Your eyes are still swollen but you're going to be fine. These stitches need to be taken out in a couple of days. You might have some slight scarring, Parker."

"Did Parker really need to stay in there for another couple of days?" Denny asked.

"Well, in my opinion, no. If the bandages were off, Parker could very easily see what she needs to do in the house. As far as driving and everything else, she needs to let someone else do that for a couple of days."

Denny and I looked at each other. Was someone at the hospital playing games? Why was I being kept there? What had I stumbled into?

"Parker, I'm here and no one, absolutely *no one*, will get to you." Denny's voice was flat. "I bought Potus with me. He's out in the camper and I'm bringing him in."

A few minutes later, Potus, which actually stands for President of the United States, bounded into the living room and came over to slather me with kisses. Even for an Akita, Potus is a little larger and more protective than most other Akitas. He loves me. We had had to use him on several different occasions and I knew he would protect me at all costs.

After a few minutes of hugging and kissing him, I took his huge head in my hands and looked into his eyes. "Potus, you need to protect me because I don't know what's going on and I don't know who to trust. You got me, buddy?" He blinked his eyes as if to say "I gotcha."

"Secure."

Potus snapped to attention on high alert at Denny's command. He immediately started going from room to room, then nothing. No woof, no clicking of his nails on my hardwood floors, just silence.

Denny wiggled his finger in a horizontal circle indicating that Doc and I were to continue talking. We were just making small talk when Denny came back into the room with his finger to his lips. He had a small button-looking thing in his hand. He gave a hand signal to Potus to keep the area secure and then went out to the camper.

Doc turned to me and said, "Parker, what have you gotten into this time?"

I was stunned. Why would someone bug my house? I wasn't even sure which room Denny and Potus had found the bug. Geez Louise, I hoped it wasn't in the bedroom. I really hoped I wasn't going to show up on the internet with me and Joe D. doing the slap and giggle game.

Denny came in a few minutes later. Grim-faced, he said, "How well do you know Joe D. and how much do you trust him?"

"What?" Was this day going to get any better? "I've known Joe D. since high school and, of course, you know we date every time I come back to Po'thole."

"His thumb print is on the bug." He paused for a moment. "It's a five point match. The bug was in your ceiling light in your office and was pointed directly at your laptop."

"But, but," I stuttered, "I don't get it. Who would want to see my laptop? They could have just as easily taken the darn thing."

Then it dawned on me. "Wait! They wanted to see what I was working on at any given time."

"Parker, not to make you feel any better but this bug had a zoom lens on it. Anything you typed on your laptop could be very easily seen and...," he cleared his throat. "It was being transmitted."

I felt sick, betrayed, and in total disbelief that Joe D. had anything to do with this. Yet, I knew Denny wouldn't lie about Joe D.'s fingerprint.

My cell phone went off for the umpteenth time. This time I looked at my caller ID and saw that it was Dewitt calling. Had to be good.

"Hi, Dewitt. What's new?"

"Parker," he paused, cleared his throat. "Parker, have you received any death threats?"

I snorted. "What? Where have you been? Didn't I bring you the one that was on my windshield the other day? Didn't someone blow up my car and almost kill me and Penny? Didn't someone in the hospital not want me to leave? Something different from that, Dewitt?"

Ignoring my sarcasm, he asked, "Have you received any death threats on your cell phone?"

"I don't know. I haven't answered it until you called."

"Cathy Jean who's doing all the real estate sales to them Arabs out in West River, she's received death threat phone calls. Since you're having so many problems, I needed to know if you're receiving calls."

"Dewitt, was it a male or female who's calling in threats to Cathy Jean?"

"She thinks it's a female."

"Do you think it's one of the Lady Gatorettes? They've been pretty vocal about locals selling their property and they're not one bit happy about it."

I could almost see the wheels spinning in Dewitt's head. "Well, you're right about that, but you know they'll never turn on each other. It sure does sound like something they'd do."

"Haul in Misty Dawn. She's going through some hormonal changes now." I chuckled. "Actually, she would make the most sense for making the call."

Dewitt whined. "She's mean, Parker. Plus, she's crazy. She might tear up the jail and I don't really have anything to arrest her on."

Really? A law enforcement officer cringing about bringing in a Lady Gatorette? I could just see Misty Dawn, Rhonda Jean, Myrtle Sue, Mary Jane, and Flo doing even more crazy things in the county knowing that law enforcement was scared of them.

"Dewitt, call Tony Bugs then and let him put the fear of God into them." My phone started beeping indicating another call was coming in. "Dewitt, I got to go. My office is calling me."

The caller ID showed it was Joe D. calling. I ignored it.

Denny said, "Let me guess, Dewitt's afraid to pick up any of the Lady Gatorettes."

I just nodded. It was one thing to make crazy phone calls, and I could honestly see any of the Lady Gatorettes doing that for a football game, but to threaten someone for doing their job? I thought that was a little out of character even for them.

"Denny, let me lay this out for you and you tell me what you think."

He nodded.

I told him about Bobby Derlicter being trussed up like a turkey and the barbeque dinner. Barbeque was the dinner of choice for Buddy Walker's and Jack Canaday's murders. I was being spied and eavesdropped on. My car was blown up. It appeared that Joe D. was perhaps involved in some way and, at the very least, had some shady dealings going on. The Lady Gatorettes seemed to be hanging out on the periphery on everything, not to mention the feud going on with Dewitt and Tony Bugs. Property being sold out in West River to Arabs who apparently had an unlimited amount of money.

I finished with, "Everyone's crazy and I don't who to trust."

"Well, you did know small towns have their fair share of craziness when you came back here."

"Yeah, but what do *you* think is going on?"

Doc Naismith popped up, "Why don't you just Google water, facing east, and Muslims? Chances are they are Muslims and something might show up for you."

I couldn't believe it! I was a tech expert and I hadn't even thought about Googling that combination. Denny was texting Missy the info. Twenty minutes later, he shook his head.

"Nothing."

"I guess I need to call Homeland Security," I said, dialing the number.

Total silence as the phone was answered. This was a little bit unusual even for my Homeland Security contact.

"Um, it's Parker. I need to talk with…"

Interrupting me, he said, "I know who it is. We want to thank you for your services and a final check will be deposited into your account."

Staring at my phone, I was surprised. Although I didn't do a whole lot for Homeland Security, it felt like my country had just dumped me.

Doc Naismith and Denny looked at me and then Denny cleared his throat. "Um, that was a pretty short phone call even for them. What's going on?"

I shook my head. "Something really strange is going on. Homeland Security just severed all ties with me. This is just weird."

"Denny, make sure everything in the office is totally secure. Run sweeps in the office and in every system we have. Run phone logs over the past forty-five days on everyone, including your line and mine. Someone may have been using them. Have we hired anyone in the past six months?"

Denny shook his head.

"Any in the past twelve months, including outsourcing?"

"I'll check with Missy."

"Is there anyone, *anyone*, either of you can think of who could or would turn on us?"

Doc looked at Denny and then me. He shook his head no. Denny had his poker face on and shook his head no.

"Parker, I need to stay here with you. I'll have Jake take care of everything in Atlanta."

I nodded. "Make sure you run a screen on Jake before you give him anything important."

I didn't want to believe anyone in my office was feeding information to Homeland Security but something sure had caused them to slam the door on my business with them. I needed to find out if we had any leaks in my office or any of our systems. We did too much business with large corporations and governmental agencies to have a leak. Even though we ran checks on our systems all the time and it was highly unlikely that new code had popped up in our system totally unnoticed, it *was* possible. My stomach rolled like I'd just dropped to the bottom of a huge wave. *Did I have a traitor in my midst?* I leaned back against the pillow Doc has propped behind me and closed my swollen eyes. Every breath made my head pound.

We vetted all of our employees every six months. While that may sound like paranoia, it's the nature of high tech computer security firms. I hired the best of the best but, unfortunately, even *they* could be swayed with the right offer.

For most of the high tech geeks, it's not about the money, it's about the challenge. Can they keep someone out of the systems, can they find who's trying to infiltrate the systems, and are they better than that anonymous person? It's all about the game. That's their psychic income, that's what drives them. The physical money? They really don't care that much about it. I had people on payroll who, if we didn't direct deposit their paychecks, would never cash them.

If someone had enticed them to find a way to infiltrate or override our system without anyone in our company noticing, then that would become the new game for them. I really hoped that hadn't happened.

******

The Homeland Security man Parker had called picked up his disposable cell phone, dialed a number, and said, "Parker's contract with us has been terminated. It's all a go."

CHAPTER TWELVE

Under Protection

There was banging on my door. After looking through the peephole, Denny announced, "It's Joe D."

I shook my head no. I simply didn't trust Joe D. right now and I didn't want to engage in a pointless discussion with him right now. He always had an excuse for everything and I simply didn't have the energy or the desire to shift the truth from his lies.

Denny opened the door and stepped out. I could hear Joe D. shouting and then a thud. Doc Naismith and I looked at each other. He looked through the peephole.

"I don't see anything, Parker."

I pointed at the window and standing to the side of the curtains we both peered out. Denny was pushing Joe D. into his car except Joe D. wasn't exactly sitting up straight behind the wheel.

Denny was on his cell phone coming back into the house. "Yeah, well, he, Joe D. was hollering at Parker and was weaving around out in her front yard. He then got back into his car and now he's slumped over. I'm guessing he might have been drinking. Y'all might want to send someone over. Yeah, thanks."

We all grinned at each other.

Doc Naismith said, "Vodka or bourbon?"

Denny winked. "He might have consumed a small bottle of bourbon between the time he took a swing at me and smacking his head on the front door. I did the right thing by placing him back in his car and calling the police for possible DUI."

We all roared with laughter. Then the mood turned somber as my cell phone rang. I didn't recognize the number on caller ID.

"Hello."

"You're a dead woman." The voice was muffled but I was sure it was a woman. Casting all cares to the wind, I took a wild chance.

"Misty Dawn, you better be careful threatening me." I held my breath.

"Who?" The voice sounded puzzled. "Parker Bell, you are a dead woman." The phone went dead.

Turning to Denny, "Could you trace it?"

He shook his head. "She wasn't on there long enough and I would bet you it's a disposable phone. Nothing would show up anyway. Did you recognize the voice?"

"No. I *do* think it was a female but whoever it was didn't seem to recognize the name Misty Dawn. But I do think it's time I called Nate."

I wasn't wild about calling the FBI but something seemed to be very off about Homeland Security, plus, it was fun to stir the pot with different national law enforcement agencies.

"Federal Bureau of Information."

"Nate Sirraca, please."

"Nate Sirraca."

"Wow! I got through to you right away. I'm impressed. It's Parker Bell."

Nate and I had history together. Nothing I had ever shared with Joe D. or even Denny, although I suspected Denny knew. Also, Nate's last name wasn't Sirraca. It was a coded last name that I used when I needed to get through to him right away. It also let him know I had others standing near me who were listening in.

"Hello, Parker, what can I do for you today?"

I quickly brought him up to speed on everything that was going on in Po'thole, focusing predominantly on the Middle Eastern connection and Homeland Security. I finished with the news that Homeland Security had summarily terminated my contract.

"Hum, you're right. None of this makes much sense, particularly the Homeland Security part. Let me make a few inquiries. Be careful." He hung up.

Denny started to laugh. Wrinkling my face up in mock horror, I started to laugh too, though it hurt like holy hell. Denny just had one of those infectious laughs that spread like wildfire. Doc Naismith tried to suppress his laughter and then suddenly fell back on the couch laughing as tears rolled down his face.

"Denny, what are we laughing about?" I finally managed to gasp after collapsing in the recliner. Laughter does a body good. I could feel the healing already.

Cocking his head to one side and doing a major eyebrow arch, he leaned forward and said, "You ought to call Saffron Woo and see what kind of advance you could get for...." He paused for effect. "For...Murder in Po'thole."

We all fell apart again, laughing at the title. The fine upstanding citizens of Po'thole would run me out of town for sure. And probably burn the family homestead that I refused to abandon completely.

"Walmartians won't let you in the store for sure." Doc Naismith was rocking back and forth on the couch with laughter.

I was laughing so hard I thought the stitches in my head would pop open by themselves. We had a few more minutes of levity and, I'll be honest, I wasn't paying any attention to what Denny was doing until a cell phone was thrust in my face.

"Hello," I managed to gasp out.

"Parker, darling, how are you?" The breathless voice of Saffron Woo managed to make me cringe even amongst the laughter. I saluted Denny with my middle finger.

"I've got a great title for my new book." I shut my almost-shut eyes, took a deep breath, and let it out slowly. And, knowing that I was going to regret it, I said, "Murder in Po'thole."

"Murder in Pothole?"

Trying to avoid looking at Denny and Doc Naismith since they were now rolling around on the couch in the death throes of murderous laughter, I managed to say, "Poat hole, like goat hole, not Pothole. Murder in Po'thole."

"Darlin' I'm on it. The next time I call it will be with good news and a wonderful, wonderful advance." Saffron Woo hung up.

Peals of laughter erupted when the cell phone rang again.

"Gosh, I'm popular," I laughed. "Hello?"

"Boom, boom, your house is doomed."

Click.

"What?" I waved my hands at the guys to stop laughing. "Hello, hello? Who is this?"

I was starting to become really concerned about my safety and well-being. The voice seemed to be the same as before. What was going on? The phone rang again.

"Hello?"

"Boom, boom, your house is doomed. Get out now." *Click.*

"Guys, I think we need to leave the house now." I told them about the second warning.

Denny immediately ran to my office, grabbed my computer and flash drives, Doc Naismith was already packed and ready to go with his medical bag. As tired as I was, adrenalin kicked me into gear. I grabbed some clothes, threw them into an overnight bag, and met the guys at my front door.

"Doc, you take the lead. Parker, you're in the middle, and I'm bringing up the rear. As soon as we get outside, it's going to be the doc in front, you right behind him, and I'll be up on your right side. We're going for the RV."

I wailed, "Don't leave Potus behind!"

"What kind of medication did you give her, Doc? I've never seen Parker get so upset about Potus. I mean, I know she loves him and all but this..." waving his hand at her, "this isn't like her at all."

"You can't leave Potus!" I wailed. "He's gotta come with us." I was getting ready to go into the ugly Oprah cry. My face scrunched up and it looked like Niagara Falls was coming out of my eyeballs.

"Parker, I would never leave Potus behind. He's going to be right next to you."

Looking us all in the eye, Denny continued, "If anyone goes down, get Parker to the RV. I'll take out whoever I need to. Let's do it."

"Wait, wait!" shouted Doc Naismith. "That means I'm the bait. Noooo! I'm a doctor, I save lives and help people."

"You don't have a current doctor's license in this state. You're expendable. Move."

Denny pushed him out the front door and I was right behind him. Clouds were lazily floating across the sky, the sun was still hot, and the Florida humidity was high enough to turn anyone into a pile of jello within minutes. I hoped I could make the RV.

Instead of scanning the area like I normally would have, I concentrated on getting to the vehicle in one piece. After being in the hospital for a couple of days, my legs weren't exactly working in the most optimum fashion and my worst fear was that I would fall down on the ground like some movie helpless female. I kept banging into Potus trying to maintain my balance. He didn't seem to mind.

We had just barely gotten inside the RV when it began to vibrate slightly. I looked at the guys, wondering what was going on, and being the inquisitive individual that I am, I looked out the window.

My whole house was vibrating. It looked like it was alive. It was swaying slightly from side to side while at the same time looked like it was bobbing up and down to some strange musical beat that only it could hear.

BOOM!

It looked like a nuclear bomb had been detonated in my house. The house exploded upward with some type of weird-looking mushroom cloud going up even higher. I blinked my eyes, not really comprehending what I was seeing. My house was gone. There was a fairly large hole in the ground but no house. The RV shook, rattled, and rolled but stayed in one piece. Potus eyed the door with "I dare you" eyes. God help anyone trying to come through that door.

"Another one bites the dust," sang Denny, merriment in his eyes. "What is it with you, Parker? You have more stuff blow up and laptops break than a Stephanie Plum novel."

Just what I wanted to be compared to, a fictional character in a bestselling series by a dynamic author. Oh, wait, I mused, that's *not* a bad thing.

"Yeah, well, I'm impressed you can read," I sniped back.

"Who's that?" Doc Naismith pointed at a figure disappearing into the woods behind my house.

Considering what I had been through the past several days, the only way I probably could identify anyone was through a sniper's scope but with the naked eye I couldn't have identified the Energizer Bunny.

I shrugged.

"Looks like a fertilizer bomb to me," stated Denny. "You might want to call Dewitt and have him round up the Lady Gatorettes. See if he can get one of them to turn on each other."

My cell phone rang. Nothing showed on caller ID.

"Hello?" I asked very cautiously.

"Get out of Po'thole. You've had all the warnings you're going to get." The call disconnected before I could reply.

Doc Naismith came over, put his arm around me, and led me over to the couch. I immediately plopped down and stretched out. My head was pounding,

I didn't feel well, and I really just wanted everyone to go away and leave me alone.

"Parker, you need rest. You're pale. You've undergone a lot in the past several days and weeks. As your doctor, I am recommending you leave this godforsaken little town for at least a week and get some rest."

Denny nodded his head in agreement. "I can take care of whatever comes up, Parker."

My cell phone rang again. I was tired of receiving so many calls from crackheads.

"What?" I screamed into the phone. "What the fon-goo do you want, now?"

I heard a man clearing his throat, "Um, Parker, it's Dewitt. I hate to ask this, but was that your house that just blew up? I'm getting calls. And the second thing is, I just got a call from Homeland Security asking me to bring you in for questioning."

"For what, Dewitt? Did I freaking blow up my own house? What does Homeland Security want with me and, more importantly, why isn't one of their people here to talk to me? Why are they using you?" Waving to Denny, I mouthed the word "coffee." I took as deep a breath as I could stand and let it out slowly.

"Dewitt, call Nate Sirraca at this number," I rattled it off to him. "Tell *him* about Homeland Security's request. Tell him I need help."

"Who is Nate Sirraca?"

"FBI, Dewitt. He's FBI and he has jurisdiction over Homeland Security. Call him." Through clenched teeth, I repeated, "Be sure you tell him I need his help."

"We'll be in touch, Parker."

I started to stand up but the room was spinning, everything became a blur, and then— nothing. I came back to life lying on the couch with a cold washcloth on my head and my feet elevated on a cushion. I felt nauseous; however, I smelled freshly brewed coffee and knew that the Big Man upstairs apparently had taken great pity on me. I stretched out my arm and felt the cup being gently placed in my hand with someone pressing my fingers around it.

A hand was still wrapped around my hand holding the coffee and I was being pulled into a sitting position on the couch. I was impressed, not one drop of that precious brown liquid spilled on me or the couch.

Slurping on that hot cup of coffee was the best thing that had happened to me all day. Getting sprung from the hospital, still worried about my eyes and head, more threatening phone calls, being rushed to the RV, my house blowing up, and now Homeland Security wanting to have me arrested—it was all just too much. Even for me.

I'm not one of those crying, helpless females you see in the movies. In fact, I've never seen *any* female act like that. All of the crazy things that had happened since coming back to Po'thole simply made me mad and, by golly, someone was going to pay for the craziness.

Halfway through my second cup of coffee, my cell phone rang again. It was Dewitt.

"Whatcha got for me, Dewitt?"

His voice was flat and authoritative. "Parker, Nate Sirraca said he's never heard of you. Stay right where you are, I'm coming over. You are under arrest per the Homeland Security Act of 2002."

I was stunned. My own government had turned against me.

CHAPTER THIRTEEN

Disowned

"Parker, sit on the couch." Doc Naismith had dived into his medical bag and was waving something under my nose. Bad news was I couldn't really smell anything because of all the damage that had been done because of the donut store bombing.

"What's going on?"

I was in shock. Being in the high tech computer security business, I knew what the government could do to people...especially those who had worked with various government agencies and were deemed no longer "necessary."

They could simply disappear or even if they were still able to work, their number one client – the government – would stop being their client which usually caused them to go into bankruptcy. Since the government was not my one and only client, I wasn't that concerned about losing them as a client. What I was concerned about was them freezing my assets which also included my company payroll.

"Parker, what's going on?" Denny looked worried.

"Freeze my assets," I mumbled.

Denny immediately called Jack, our comptroller, and told him what was going on. I could hear him mumbling something into the phone. The room was starting to spin again and my cell phone went off for the umpteenth time. I couldn't believe it. My cell phone had never rung this much since the day I had started using cell phones.

"Yeah?" I was doing away with niceties since it didn't seem to get me anywhere.

"Parker?" It was a tentative female voice. "Is this Parker Bell?"

"Yeah, who's this? And please don't tell me my house or car is going to blow up. You're too late—I no longer *have* a house or a car."

"Parker, it's Rhonda Jean. We hear you're having problems and we decided—that is the Lady Gatorettes—because you were nice to us in high school, we have decided to be your bodyguards. We got your back, girl."

Oh, good lord. Has the world disintegrated to the point where the only people who want to hang around me are five hormonal, probably certifiable, crazy women? Heck, they would probably get an adrenaline rush stronger than the caffeine and sugar rush they so often enjoyed.

Apparently I had a case of the terminal DA's – terminal dumb ass - when I opened my mouth. "Rhonda Jean, you know Dewitt thinks you guys are the ones behind all of this, don't you?"

I heard a hissing sound through my phone. I pulled it away from my head thinking it was totally possible that I had a snake loose on the phone. What with everything else that was going on in my life, nothing was impossible.

"The man is history." Rhonda Jean hissed into the phone.

Sighing, I turned to the guys. "I think I just unleashed the Lady Gatorettes on Dewitt. God help him."

The guys just started smiling and Denny hopped in the front seat of the RV, started it up, and began to pull away from my newly blown-up yard.

Doc Naismith was a little nervous. "Um, if the RV is moved, doesn't that make for a fleeing from justice charge for Parker?"

"Nope." Denny turned his head back around to look at us, eyes twinkling, and laughter crinkles around his mouth. "I'm moving us away from a known demolition area and crime scene for safety reasons. I'm just going to the end of the street."

Full blown laughter burst from Denny. "Let's see how long it takes Dimwit to figure out we're just a half a block away."

I must have fallen asleep again. Next thing I knew, my cell phone started playing "Living on a Prayer" by Bon Jovi. I really needed to change my phone tune. It was becoming too true for comfort.

Denny answered it this time. "Parker Bell's phone." He nodded his head a couple of times and then started to laugh. "Dewitt, look south and you'll see us sitting at the end of the block. We are not absconding from justice. The RV needed to be moved for safety reasons. In case you haven't noticed, Parker's house was blown up and we were taking precautionary measures in case another bomb went off." He ended the call and tossed my phone on the couch.

"Dimwit couldn't find us. Parker, tell me again how this guy came to be sheriff." Snapping his fingers, he said, "Oh, yeah, that's right; he only won by four votes."

Banging on the RV door made me jump. Potus growled. Out of all the times I'd helped the United States government with computer security, they were now arresting me on suspicion of terrorism under the Homeland Security Act.

I probably should have been scared, and I *was* a little bit, but I was more angry than anything else. Plus, it was a real slap in the face to have someone like Dewitt arrest me. In fact, it really made me wonder if this was for real. I sure wasn't going to make it easy for Dewitt, though.

Denny opened the door and stood to the side, his eyes scanning the scene in front of him. I saw a slight smile twitch on his face—until he saw Potus smiling—with drool falling from his tongue.

Dewitt's head suddenly snapped forward like he had been hit in the head. He had. As he fell into the RV I could see a pink splotch on the back of his head. My brain was trying to process the color *pink* versus the color *red*.

The illustrious SWAT team broke ranks and turned around to see what caused Dewitt to fall forward. Every one of them relaxed their weapon's pose and turned to look around. The next minute all hell broke as the SWAT guys came under attack.

Pink splats of paint appeared on their uniforms and then a small canister flew through the air and landed at their feet. There was a one second pause and then it exploded spewing pink paint everywhere. The SWAT team was now in the middle of a major fashion crisis. Pink and camouflage does not look good on a bunch of beer-bellied good ol' boys who are playing at being machismo law enforcement guys.

Colorful language could be heard from all of the SWAT team members. Dewitt stood up, looking totally befuddled. His brain wasn't processing what he was seeing. He scratched his head, spreading the pink from the paintball pellet around on his head.

Denny, Doc Naismith, and I all burst out laughing. There was no doubt in my mind that the Lady Gatorettes were behind this. They didn't like Dewitt to begin with and my senseless comment that he thought *they* were behind all of this just made them want to wreak havoc on River County's finest. I knew deep down inside there would be more pink paint attacks.

Denny, wiping tears of laughter from his eyes, turned to us. "I guess they decided orange and blue paint pellets would be too much of a giveaway."

Dewitt turned to us and asked, "Now who do you think would do that to us? Pink? Are you kidding?"

The stupidity of the question just about caused me to wet my pants with laughter and the next thing I heard caused me to let loose.

Via a bullhorn from the edge of the trees came, "Boom shack-a-lacka, boom shack-a-lacka."

I was almost hysterical with laughter as was Denny and Doc Naismith. The SWAT team and Dewitt—not so much.

"You're under arrest, Parker."

"Stay, Potus." Wiping the tears from my eyes, I merely stuck my arms out waiting for Dewitt to cuff me. Apparently catching him off-guard with my Southern charm and cooperation, he just stared at my wrists. No cuffs were being applied. I shrugged, eased down the RV steps, and got into his car.

"Denny, get Marcus on this."

I enjoyed playing Driving Miss Daisy to the county jail. My rights had not been read. Nothing was said that indicated I was being arrested. I was just riding in the backseat of the sheriff's car. My attorney was going to have a field day with all of this.

Sitting in Dewitt's office sipping on some of Gloria's coffee, the pink-splattered Dewitt finally spoke. "We got a problem."

I did not respond. I didn't figure I was part of his "we."

"Parker, I said we got us a problem."

I just sat and looked at his desk while drinking my cup of coffee.

He slammed his hand on his desk. "Gosh almighty, Parker! Didn't you hear me? I said we got us a problem."

"Which is what, Dewitt?" I was going to play it out as long as possible. Good thing he couldn't see me smirking on the inside. And too bad my head felt like it was being attacked by baseball bats from the inside.

"It's those Lady Gatorettes again. They're outta control. Their wimpy husbands won't do anything about them, they keep creating havoc, and they shot up my guys with pink paint. *Pink* paint!" Dewitt's face had turned a deep red hue. I vaguely wondered if he was having a high blood pressure attack. This time I had the good sense to be quiet. Plus, I knew it would make Dewitt go off the charts. I was right.

He screamed, "Parker! Pink paint on my men! What are you going to do about it?"

Since my eyes, my nose and my head all hurt like hell from all the laughter, I kept my voice quiet and even. The voice that came out of me due to the packing and bandages on my nose made me think of a cartoon character and I almost laughed despite the pain.

"I'm not the sheriff and there's nothing I can do about them anyway, Dewitt." I leaned back in my chair and thought this would have been a good time for a cigarette but since I didn't smoke my brain went to its happy place instead. Some might call it dissociative behavior. I call it daydreaming. I was in the Bahamas lying in a hammock thinking of guys bringing me high octane rum drinks with tiny little umbrellas in them and the guys in their very tight speedos when Dewitt screamed at me again.

Opening my eyes and seeing Dewitt with foam flecks of spit on his mouth did not inspire me to go to the ocean any time soon. I returned to my happy place while Dewitt continued to have an attack of the seven fat, ugly women at a pig pit.

It suddenly dawned on me that Homeland Security didn't want me arrested. They merely wanted me out of the way, but, for what? Everything really boiled down to the Middle Eastern guys—had to be. That's why they'd sent me to Po'thole in the first place

"I'm done, Dewitt. See you later." I stood up, walked out of his office, out of the building, and got into Denny's car before Dewitt could respond. I guess he was in shock.

Denny cocked an eyebrow at me and handed me a coffee. "Is he still living or did you kill him in his own office?"

"He's living. Take me to Jazz's. I'm going to set up a meeting with those Middle Eastern guys."

Walking into the empty convenience store the same blond surfer guy was standing behind the counter. His eyes narrowed slightly.

I put on my no-nonsense face, which is not much different from my pissed-off face, slapped my hands down on the counter, leaned forward, and said, "I don't who you are or who your boss is but tell him I want to meet with him tomorrow morning at nine o'clock. Tell him I'm tired of screwing around and I want to meet him personally."

"Or what?"

"Or you and your store won't be here after ten tomorrow morning. Here's my number." I slapped my business card down. "Call my cell phone to confirm it."

I started punching my cell phone numbers as soon as I had left the store. "Find some of that property out in West River, Missy."

Then I dialed another number. "Yeah, get me Nate Sirraca. Tell him it's Parker and I'm pissed." I was chewing on my lower lip while waiting for him to pick up.

A female voice came back on the line. "We don't have a Nate Sirraca."

My brain froze. Either I was totally *persona non gratis* or something had happened to him. I didn't want to risk using his real name, even though I trusted Denny. I didn't want all of my cards exposed.

If they weren't so sore, I'd have rubbed my eyes. "Okay, how about John Sykes? Can I speak with him?"

"One moment." Almost immediately she came back on the line. "John Sykes is not with our office."

"Director John Sykes is not with the FBI any longer?" I was stunned. "Wait! Is he in another office?"

"Ma'am, we do not have a John Sykes listed for this office. Is there anything else I can help you with?"

"Do you have a John Sykes listed in any office?"

There was a pause. "No."

I hung up the phone. What was happening? John had been with the FBI for twenty years. I knew it wasn't time for retirement. I felt like I was freefalling without a parachute.

I hadn't been paying attention to where Denny was driving until we rolled up to a hangar at the Po'thole Municipal Airport. He jumped out as the hangar door rolled up. Once Doc drove the RV inside, Denny jumped back in the car, did a three-point turn, and backed the car in next to the RV.

Opening my car door, he said, "We're safe here. We're on the west side of the airport, we can't be seen from the road, and no one else has rented any hangars on this side. It's all ours.

"You need rest...badly. Turn off your cell phone. Whatever happens tonight can wait until tomorrow."

"You're under my care now, Parker." Doc Naismith popped his head out of the inside office door. "There's a shower in here. Take one and we'll have dinner in the RV when you get out."

Grinning, he said, "The shower's bigger in here than in the RV. I've put some clothes on the chair for you. Denny put tint on the windows. No one can see inside or even see light from the outside. You are completely safe and we'll be in the RV with dinner for you when you get out."

I just nodded, overwhelmed with the thoughtfulness of my guys. Good thing neither one of them appealed to me in a Biblical sense sort of way; otherwise, naughty things might happen during the night.

Relaxing in a hot, luxurious shower after what I had been through was a joyous gift. I could feel the day's nastiness being rinsed from my body and going down the drain. I stayed in the shower until the water started turning cold.

Entering the RV, the smell of good, hot food was overwhelming. My mouth started to drool. Denny set a plate down in front of me. We all scarfed down the food and went back for seconds. I took the pills Doc Naismith handed me and was almost out on my feet before I stumbled into the bedroom.

The *boom* I vaguely heard outside the hangar door didn't even get me out of bed.

CHAPTER FOURTEEN

Pink Camo

Fourteen hours later, I woke up not knowing where I was. I wandered out into the main area of the RV and saw sunshine through the front windows. Since I knew we were supposed to be in the hangar where sunlight did not penetrate the walls, I was perplexed and a little uneasy.

"What's up, guys?" I was on the hunt for coffee. Both Denny and Doc Naismith were huddled over a laptop on what was supposed to be a kitchen pull-out table.

Denny hadn't shaved and looked a little on the haggard side. Doc Naismith looked like he had been rode hard and hung up wet.

Looking up at me, Denny said, "Didn't you hear anything last night?"

Shaking my head no, he glared at Doc. "What the heck did you give her?"

"Just something to help her sleep."

"She's been out for fourteen hours, Doc. She doesn't know anything about last night. Why..."

"Guys," I interrupted them while slurping down some coffee, "what's going on? I see sunlight. I thought we were in the hangar and, I'm assuming here, something happened so that we had to leave. What's going on?"

Denny rubbed the top of his head with both hands. "There was an explosion outside the hangar door. Some gunfire."

I interrupted him. "Gunfire? Are you kidding? I didn't hear a thing. Who was it?"

"Really, doc, did you have to give her something so strong?" Denny glared at Doc. Doc ignored Denny.

"Well, there was gunfire, then banging on the hangar door." He paused for a moment. "Then a female voice shouted 'clear' and then, 'go now.' I can only assume it was the Lady Gatorettes who came to our rescue. I opened the door and we drove out."

Doc Naismith jumped in and said, "There were a couple of dead bodies on the ground and several people in pink fatigues dragging them off."

He cleared his throat. "It was definitely females doing the dragging."

"What the heck happened?" I was beyond surprised at the latest turn of events.

"Don't know. What's even scarier is how did anyone know where we were? I swept the RV for bugs, inside and out, before we ever left the sheriff's office. We never stopped and there were no tails."

"Could someone have run a check on any of our cell phones and found us that way?"

"That's a possibility," Denny admitted reluctantly.

"But the real question is why am I so important that someone would want to do that?" I knew it wasn't one of my business competitors. Heck, they were probably thrilled that I wasn't in Atlanta at the moment. "What have we stumbled onto that we're not supposed to know?"

Pondering the situation for a few moments, although not a brilliant deduction on my part, I said, "Everything goes back to the Middle Eastern guys. Somehow they are the key to all of this. Bobby Derlicter, Buddy Walker, and Happy Jack must have known something without actually being aware that they knew something. Seriously, guys, I'm supposed to have a one-to-one meeting with these foreigners. If for no other reason than to tell them I'm not trying to bring them down or stop whatever it is they're doing out in West River.

"Denny, take me over to that convenience store right now. This has got to stop. By, the way, I need more coffee."

Thank goodness, I almost had Doc totally trained to get my coffee without asking because he jumped up to get me more coffee while muttering, "Sorry, sorry."

A few minutes later we were at the convenience store. Blond surfer dude looked up from the magazine he was reading at the counter. He jerked his thumb toward the Employee Only door. "He's in there."

"Nope. The last time I went through that door I got bonked on the head. You go through first."

The guy shrugged, walked to the door, opened it, stuck his head inside, and said, "She's here and she ain't coming inside."

A tall guy with thick black hair and a beard came to the doorway. "I'm who you want to talk to. Come on back — you're safe."

He smiled slightly. "I promise."

I was a wee bit apprehensive but decided to take the plunge anyway. I had put on my Captain Marvel ring, or that's what I called it, and if I pushed on the center of it for more five seconds, Denny would come charging through the door. A girl always needs backup and a Plan B.

"What's going on? Why are you guys chasing and threatening me? Why are local people being killed?" I demanded.

"First, let me introduce myself to you. I'm Amir Mossaui. I am from Iran and, yes," he smiled slightly. "I am a U.S. citizen. I am also a developer of property."

"Great, congratulations on being a U.S. citizen." Okay, so I had my snarky moments. "What's going on? Why all the secrecy? Why all the murders? In short, just *why*?"

Amir's black eyes felt like they were peering into my soul. I blinked first. He smiled again. "What if I told you that West River and Po'thole were about to explode with new business?"

"I'd say great, but I'm still asking what's going on?"

Turning to a large map taped to the wall, Amir said, "You see all these lakes?"

I nodded.

"You see the yellow showing all of the properties I have purchased?" He looked to me. I nodded again.

"You see everything points east, to Mecca, right? This is my way of honoring my god and my forefathers—the ones who made it possible for me to be here today."

Turning back to me, he asked, "Do you know anything about these lakes?"

I shook my head no.

"They are known for exceptional fishing. The lakes are very easy to re-stock with fish. The properties are easy to get to...either by driving or by flying into the Po'thole Municipal Airport. What's even better is there will be beautiful fishing cabins for families on some of the lakes. On other lakes, there will be some just for men and some just for women. People will be able to fish from shore, from boats in the lakes, and if someone doesn't like fishing, there will be a small movie cinema at the main clubhouse. Do you see where I'm going with this?"

Without thinking, I blurted out, "You're creating a fishing Disney World!"

He smiled. "Miss Bell, I think you understand now what I am doing. If I tell people what I am doing up front, the property will cost much, much more. Think of how many people and companies I will be hiring to do this work. It is very, very good for everyone."

"But why Po'thole? Why not closer to a larger city?"

"Because what River County offers is far superior to anything anywhere close to here. The natives overlook the very things that make it wonderful for others to see...the nature, the fishing, the lakes, family values. You see what I am offering to the nice people here?" He waved his hands.

"What about the murders of Bobby Derlicter, Buddy Walker, and Happy Jack Canaday? What did they ever do to you?"

"Miss Bell, I had nothing to do with them. I do not know who killed them. I'm in the dark about that as well."

"So why is Homeland Security so interested in you?" The whole puzzle was becoming stranger and stranger. The pieces just weren't fitting together.

He smiled. "Look at me. I stand out in a crowd. Also, people of Middle Eastern descent are being watched very carefully because of possible terrorism. I have done very well financially in this country, that alone makes me suspect.

"I assure you, all this is about is developing a 'fishing Disney World,' as you put it. I will help your people and some of mine as well. I could care less about anything else."

I wasn't sure if I believed him but I didn't have any proof otherwise.

"The word will soon be getting out about what I am going to do because I've purchased all the property I need. The hiring for the construction work will start next week."

Taking a shot in the dark, I asked, "Why did a couple of your men try to blow up the airplane hangar I was in last night?"

He seemed startled. "I don't know anything about that. Just a moment." He tapped his cell phone and spoke in Farsi to someone. Me, who can only speak Southern and English, had absolutely no clue as to what he was saying. For all I knew, he could have been ordering my demise.

"I know nothing about this." His tone was flat and I didn't believe him.

Standing up, I said, "So, you have no problem with me telling law enforcement that you are creating a fishing development."

"Do what you think you have to do. I will continue my plans."

Leaving the store, I still had about a hundred-million questions running loose in my head. I had some answers but not enough to actually figure out what was going on. I relayed all of the information to Denny. He didn't have a clue either and was also one hundred percent sure that the dead guys were Middle Easterners. He was just as sure that the Lady Gatorettes were the ones who had killed them. Depending upon what time of the month it was, the dead guys would never be found or they would be left on the courthouse lawn as a warning. You just never knew with those hormonal gals.

"Let's go see Dewitt and tell him what I've found out."

"Probably not a good idea, Parker. Remember, he's still upset that you walked out of his office a free woman."

"Ah, yes, but now he can spread the word that a fishing developer is in the area and that will help to alleviate some of the nasty rumors floating around town. It shows that he's on top of things."

Denny snorted, "Yeah, anyone who knows him is going to believe *that*. They're going to believe someone fed him that information."

I shrugged. "And your point would be what? With him putting the word out, it will spread like wildfire and it may flush out some other folks so we can find out what's going on. Parts of this whole thing make sense, but other parts don't seem to connect with anything. I don't understand why Homeland Security is involved, I don't understand why I've been drop kicked out, I don't understand what's happened to Nate. I mean he's been with the FBI for years."

My cell phone rang. "Hello."

"Parker, we've got your back."

"Wait!" I shouted. "Why did you kill the guys in front of the hangar last night? How did you know that's where I was?"

A slight pause, then, "They had a rocket launcher aimed at the hangar. There's an app to track your phone. Geez, Parker, you oughta know that. We got your back."

I looked at the dead phone. "Denny, I thought if the GPS was turned off on my phone, I couldn't be tracked. One of the Lady Gatorettes just told me there's an app to track the cell phone number. Is that true?"

He nodded. "Yep, but I thought the Atlanta crew had scrambled your system so that couldn't happen. I'll check and find out what's going on."

I mused, "You know, what if it's one of the Lady Gatorettes who killed Bobby, Buddy, and Happy Jack? What would the reason be?"

Dialing the donut shop—yes, I had them on speed dial—I tapped my fingers nervously on my pants leg. "Hey, Penny, it's Parker. Yeah, I'm good. Hey, what do any of the Lady Gatorettes have against Bobby or Buddy or Happy Jack? Well, yeah, I'll come over to your place. I need some coffee anyway."

Denny had already started to head for the donut shop. "I'm guessing there may be some sort of connection there."

Arriving a few minutes later, we walked up to the counter where Penny put down two steaming hot cups of the nectar of the gods, coffee. She leaned over the counter and looked conspiratorially at me and said, "We need to talk. In my office. Give me five and then just come on back."

Geez, Louise, I thought. I wondered if Penny was in on whatever was going on, too. I almost immediately pushed that thought from my head. She was still mad at the girls from when they had trashed her place. Of course, she probably wasn't any happier with me since my car blew up in front of her store and busted the plate glass window. I did notice it had been replaced.

A few minutes later I had another fresh cup of coffee and was sitting in Penny's closet-size office. She was sitting behind her desk nervously tapping a pencil on her desk. She looked like she was wrestling with what to tell me.

Finally, she looked up at me, then bowed her head and said, "You know how the Lady Gatorettes are about joining in on a conversation? And you know how they are in general, right?"

I nodded my head. On the best of days, the Lady Gatorettes were scary and when they got upset it was very definitely an all-for-one, one-for-all mentality. If they had gone into the military they would have all been black ops within a week. I don't think even the government could have controlled them. World War Three would have broken out somewhere.

"Well, they were in here one day and Misty Dawn was over the edge about how Bobby wouldn't say hello to her in the grocery store. Apparently she followed him around the store asking him why he wouldn't say hello to her. And," Penny paused, looking up, "she was quite loud and the store manager asked her to leave. She did and on the way to her car she passed by Bobby's truck. Apparently she fell into the truck and her keys somehow, magically, wrote 'your a dead man' on the door."

"Why haven't I heard about this before now? I mean what about Dewitt or Tony Buggs questioning her?"

"Well, Parker, Bobby didn't report it. Obviously, he wasn't too concerned about it. Plus, he took the truck to Mike's and had them buff and repaint the truck. He got the insurance company to pay for it because it was vandalism. Even though he knew who had done it, he couldn't prove it because no one saw Misty Dawn actually do it."

I nodded. It made perfect sense to me.

"Then," Penny continued, "they were in here another day, talking and yacking as usual, when I heard Misty Dawn say 'he's gotta die.' I looked over at them, they were being really loud at that point, and they all looked like Bambi in the headlights. Rhonda Jean says they were talking about that bull of Misty Dawn's. Myrtle Sue, Flo, and Mary Jane all nodded their heads but I knew something was up so I just went back to waiting on customers and cleaning the counter—but I was keeping my ears open."

I nodded. This was getting good. "Could I get some more coffee, Penny?"

She scurried out the door. Things were starting to make sense to me now. Misty Dawn always had the quickest temper and always thought people were out to get her. Since she hated Bobby because of the whole episode years ago about the Lady Gatorettes wanting to join the Gator Club and not being allowed to, she always had a major chip on her shoulder about him.

But would she resort to murder over something so trivial? That I didn't know for sure, although I didn't think it would take much to have her consider it. For her to actually take another human being's life, I just didn't know. In all honesty, I was probably afraid to let my thoughts go down that path.

Penny came back in with a fresh cup of coffee and picked up right where she left off. "Then I heard them talking about going to Buddy's for lunch and that's when all heck broke loose. Misty Dawn jumped up and screamed at Flo and Myrtle Sue, something about Buddy wouldn't name a sandwich after them and she wasn't gonna eat there. Ah, she was doing quite a bit of cussing. Anyway, she threw a doughnut at Rhonda Jean and stomped out.

"The rest of them just sat there. I think they were as surprised about the outburst as I was. Then I heard Flo say 'you don't think she's going to do anything about this, do you?' They all looked at me and I pretended I didn't hear them. They left shortly after that."

"Penny, you don't think Misty Dawn would actually *kill* someone do you? I mean, I thought all of these murders had to do with that new fishing development out in West River."

Penny's ears perked right up. "What new fishing development? There's foreigners buying up property. What are you talking about?"

She had taken the bait, pun intended.

"It's true. I had a meeting with the developer this morning and what's going on out there is that he's going to be doing something like a fishing Disney World where families can go fishing and have fun. There's going to be a lake just for guys and one just for folks without kids. Should be a really nice development." I smiled, taking a drink from my mug. "It should really boost the economy here…including *your* business."

"Really? That's what's going on?" Penny started grinning. "When are new crews coming in? I need to be prepared for a lot of new business."

"Well, he told me he was going to start next week. I'd probably give it more like two weeks and your products don't go bad either, do they?"

"The doughnut stuff doesn't." She started to clap her hands, "Oh, this is so good."

"By the way, whatever happened with the security crew at the Bigby plant? What was that all about?"

She frowned, trying to recall. "Oh, that. They only came for a couple of weeks because they were training to do security for a bigger power plant. Our guys were training them."

She sighed, "They were cute though."

"The Lady Gatorettes?" I prompted.

"Oh, yeah. The girls came in kinda giggly because Misty Dawn had decided to get a car. A used one, mind you, but a car."

"I thought she was totally a truck person."

"Apparently, they thought so too and the deal about Misty Dawn getting a car indicated, to them anyway, that she might be changing up on her redneck ways. Mainly because you can't tote a shotgun on the back window of a car and you know how Misty Dawn likes that Mossberg shotgun."

I nodded. The girl did have an obsession with Mossbergs. She considered them to be ideal guns, particularly the Mossberg riot shotgun with pistol grips and ventilated rib. I loved them too. Bless her heart, she almost drooled when talking about her gun. She had named it Howard.

"She went to see Happy Jack and told him she wanted to buy a car. He told her cars weren't for women like her. She needed another truck and he'd be happy to sell her one. She insisted that she wanted a car and then he poked fun at her. And you know that Misty Dawn don't take a joke well."

Not take a joke well? *That was the understatement of the century!*

"He might not have even said much of anything but she construed it as making fun of her. So they were back in here shortly after her visit with him and she said he was going to be anything but happy when she finished with him."

"Penny, did any of the other Lady Gatorettes appear to be upset with what she was saying?"

"Parker," she sighed, "do you have any idea how many times I've heard someone threaten to kill someone, especially the Lady Gatorettes? You just kinda take these things with a grain of salt. I didn't pay no never mind to it. Well, until the guys were all dead and then I kinda wondered but I really just never thought Misty Dawn might actually follow through on any of it."

Wiping her eyes, she said, "I might have been wrong."

CHAPTER FIFTEEN

Living On A Prayer

As Penny was talking, the pieces of the puzzle finally started to drop into place.

"Penny, would any of the other Lady Gatorettes ever help Misty Dawn to do that? If they knew she did, would they ever report her to Dewitt or Tony Buggs?" I knew the answer but wanted to see how honest Penny was in her assessment.

"I don't think so on the murders. They might help her cover up, but commit an actual murder? No, I don't think so. As to Dewitt or Tony Buggs?" She laughed. "You already know the answer to that."

My cell phone rang. Penny started to laugh, "'Living on a Prayer'? That's funny, Parker, and you definitely need it!"

"Hello," I answered cautiously.

"Meet me at the city dock in ten minutes." *Click.* What was wrong with all these people who gave me orders and then just hung up? Had they gone to the Ernestine the Telephone Operator School of Poor Manners?

I had recognized the voice. It was John Sykes—my Nate Sirraca. What was he doing in town?

Since nothing in Po'thole is more than seven minutes away including one end of town to the other, I arrived at the city dock a few minutes later. The only thing I saw was a bass boat being launched.

Walking up to the boat, I recognized John. He was in baggy, tourist shorts and a flowered shirt.

"John, what is going on?" I looked hard at him. "You owe me that much."

He nodded. "Let's go for a ride."

"Oh, heck, no I'm not getting in a bass boat with you and go out on that river. You decide to push me out, the water moccasins or gators will get me before I get to shore. Not happening."

I was adamant. I had seen what cottonmouth moccasins could do to a human being and it wasn't pretty. I wasn't in the mood to be gator hors d'oeuvres either. "I'm also not sitting on the edge of the dock with you either.

We can either sit on the bench on the dock, keeping in mind that voices float across the water and people can hear what we're saying, or we can sit at the picnic tables over there." I pointed at the picnic pavilion.

He nodded, tossed some keys to a guy who suddenly stood up on the other side of the bass boat. "Alright, picnic tables it is."

We didn't speak until we were facing each other across the table. I had my back to the river. I wasn't sure I trusted John anymore. Heck, I wasn't sure I trusted anyone anymore. I pressed the center of the ring I was wearing. I couldn't see him but I knew Denny was already in sniper range if something happened to me. John would be dead before I hit the ground. I also knew Denny had been watching the whole thing through his gun scope and had seen the guy stand up on the other side of the boat. He would be dead also and neither one of their bodies would ever be found, if it came to that. Once a black op, always a black op.

"Parker," John's eyes bored straight into mine, "we have a leak in the FBI."

"Oh, why, doesn't that surprise me?" I sarcastically remarked.

He held up his hand. "Just a second, let me finish. Although we sort of keep an eye on large blocks of property being purchased throughout the United States, unless there is a real reason to look at it more closely, we pretty much ignore it. That's Homeland Security's area and we already know some of those guys are just looking for reasons to confiscate property. They want to make a splash to the American public that they are actually doing something—justify their existence."

"Do you even know why this man is buying up the property or is this just another wild goose chase by the United States government?"

John cocked his head. "You need to be careful about saying things like that. Remember, you *work* for the government."

"No, actually, I don't, John." I replied hotly. "Homeland Security terminated my contract—by phone. Then they told the Sheriff to arrest me. You denied you knew me, and then you up and disappear from the FBI. I'm not real sure who you are, who you work for, or if I can trust you anymore.

"As far as the wild goose chase thing goes, yeah, I've done work for the government and I'll also tell you a lot of their 'investigations' are simply pure nosiness. It has nothing, repeat, *nothing* to do with *any* national security issue.

"So, buddy," I said sarcastically, "what's going on?"

Something shifted in the air, the universe. Maybe a guardian angel's wings warned me. Call it whatever you want, but in that split second I knew in my heart I was going to be killed. I tapped three times on my ring and then rolled onto my left shoulder semi-under the picnic table.

I never heard the gunshot but heard a whoosh of air from John and knew he was dead. A couple of seconds later I heard Denny. "Clear."

Standing up, I looked around to see where Denny was. He was trotting up to me from the bass boat.

Concern was etched all over his face. "You okay, Parker?"

"Yes," I nodded. "I'm assuming you got the other one, too."

"Yep," he looked around to make sure we hadn't attracted unwanted attention. Thankfully, there wasn't anyone around. "Where do you want me to dispose them?"

"I'm thinking we might call Tony Buggs and let him handle it." I saw Denny's eyebrow arch slightly. "But I really think I need to call the FBI's Jacksonville office and see what they want done."

"Think you're opening up a can of worms on this, Parker?"

"Maybe, but I still have a couple of aces in the hole, Denny, and, if need be, we can always disappear for awhile. The office can run by itself and as long as I have a laptop, we're plugged in. No big deal."

"Keeping you in laptops might be problematic from underground," Denny said dryly. Since he'd just saved my life, I didn't punch him or offer to fire him. I dialed my cell phone instead.

"FBI."

I sat down on the concrete table bench, suddenly very tired. "Hi, who do I need to talk to about the death of one of your agents?"

Never missing a beat, the girl responded, "One moment, please."

Less than three seconds later a man was on the line. "This is Tom Berger. What about one of our people?"

He was no nonsense and there was absolutely no doubt in my mind that the call was being recorded and traced. I knew I was out on a limb and hoped for the best.

I told him what I knew and finished with John and his partner's death. I held my breath and wished I had a cup of coffee.

"Where are the bodies?"

"Uh, Tom, not so quick? What's going on here and don't tell me it's national security. I have a Q security clearance."

"Just a moment."

I heard a series of clicks and his voice came back on the line. "Okay, I had to put us on a secure line, Parker. Yes, I know who you are and, yes, I know what's going on down in Pothole."

"It's Po'thole, just like *goat* with a hole," I interrupted him.

"Okay, down in Po'thole. There may have been collusion between John and someone in Homeland Security. We are working on finding out who that individual is. As to the reason, we believe they are part of a terrorist cell and were going to use River County as a wake-up call to the rest of the country that if a small town or area in rural Florida could be vulnerable, then so would the rest of the United States."

"How long have you known this about John? I must say I am really, really surprised."

"John walked out of the office a couple days ago, left his car in a mall parking lot, didn't go home, and was, basically, off the grid. We weren't sure where he was. When you called and asked first for Nate and then John, that triggered everything. I strongly suspected he would be headed your way because you were getting too close to the truth."

"But, wait," I protested, "I really don't know much of anything. The only thing I've really figured out is that it's probably one of the Lady Gatorettes who's murdered three people, not the Middle Eastern guys."

He interrupted me, "And why do you think that is, Parker?"

As scary as the Lady Gatorettes were, I didn't really want to throw them under the bus. Due process of law and all that. I also didn't want the remainder of them stalking me and then deciding to take revenge if I turned one of them in.

"Probably because one of them felt slighted by the guys and she is, umm, somewhat hormonal on her best days. Maybe she just had a bad day...or several of them."

I heard a slight chuckle. "Parker, don't worry, we don't care about them. That's a local matter. What we are really concerned with is sabotage on that new fishing development and then during the grand opening, which I think is projected to be in about eight months, is having hundreds if not a thousand people injured. It would be equivalent to the Boston Marathon bombing. That's what we don't want happening."

"Yeah, but that's Homeland Security's job, right?"

"Normally yes, but we've had this rogue agent go off the grid and we don't know what he was planning or who he was in contact with. That's the reason we're now involved. I need to get those bodies back...with all of their belongings, like their wallets."

"So you just want me to tell you where you can pick them up?"

"Yes. By the way, did you find anything of interest in their wallets?"

I rolled my eyes. "No."

"And you did put everything back in the wallets, right?"

I laughed. "Of course. I'm not going to be charged with anything, am I?"

"No."

Then I told him where he could find the bodies.

Denny and I decided to have lunch at The Capt'n's Table where I filled him in on everything.

Shaking his head, he said, "There's still too many loose ends on this thing. Something doesn't make sense with the Homeland Security and FBI connection. I'm going to make some phone calls after lunch." He took another bite of his lunch.

"What are you going to do about the Lady Gatorettes?" He nodded toward the door as they loudly entered The Capt'n's Table.

Various shout outs of, "Hey, Parker" rang out as they tromped past our table. I smiled and nodded.

Inside I was cringing. If Misty Dawn had truly murdered Bobby, Buddy, and Happy Jack, one more wouldn't make a difference. The death penalty was still the death penalty. I sure didn't want to be victim number four and, to be fair, the evidence on her, at best, was circumstantial. I was pretty sure she didn't keep any souvenirs pinning her to the murders and I was just as sure that none of the other Lady Gatorettes would turn on her.

Before I could answer Denny, Dewitt and his merry SWAT team band came charging through the door wearing gas masks. They tossed a tear gas canister at the Lady Gatorettes.

Unfortunately, it hit Myrtle Sue in the back and she had the re-action time of a monkey on steroids. Although it had been many years since Myrtle Sue had tried out for the semi-pro baseball team in Lakeland, she grabbed the canister before it started spewing out its noxious fumes and absolutely drilled it into Dewitt's crotch. Although he was behind the SWAT team, he stood off to the side thereby making him an open target since he didn't have a shield in front of him. He dropped like a stone.

Whipping a yellow nylon rope out of her purse, Flo tossed an end to Rhonda Jean and they charged the SWAT team. Totally not expecting *anyone* to charge them, the lead guy with the shield hesitated just a moment too long.

Flo and Rhonda Jean had fanned out, stretching the rope tight between the two of them, ducked down to ankle level, and swept the lead guy's feet out from under him. As he started to fall, the rest of the team's forward momentum caused them to fall as well. Shouting and cursing, Dewitt's pride and joy were all laying in a heap on the floor. Flo and Rhonda Jean raced out the door.

The Florida Fish and Wildlife Commission officers chose the wrong time to make an entrance from the St. Johns River. Misty Dawn, Myrtle Sue, and Mary Jane escaped by pushing the guys out of the way, jumped in their boat, and went up the St. Johns River.

It was bad enough that Denny and I already had tears pouring down our face from the teargas, having the SWAT team see us laughing hysterically at the turn of events caused tremendous humiliation to their male ego that was probably going to take years of liquid therapy to undo.

Dewitt was still laying on the floor moaning. Denny and I decided it was time to leave.

******

Several months later, I was being interviewed on the television talk show, "Really?" The host Karen Sokrates, leaned forward, tilted her head and arched her right eyebrow.

"Parker, your New Times bestseller, A Dose of Nice, has murder, suspense, terrorism, conspiracy between the FBI and Homeland Security, and a bunch of crazy women on the loose. *Really?*"

Laughing, I said, "Really. It's true, *all* of that did happen. An FBI agent did go rogue and teamed up with an agent from Homeland Security in an effort to show the weaknesses within our country. Misguided though they were, they were trying to get additional funding for their respective agencies. The poor Middle Eastern guy was really trying to do something good for everyone."

Taking a deep breath, and knowing full well the Lady Gatorettes were watching the show, I said, "As to the crazy women you referred to, they are die-hard University of Florida Gator fans. Go Gators!" I did my best Gator chomp.

I watched Karen's eyebrow arch a little higher. We both knew this was going to be a highly watched show.

"Anyway, they call themselves the Lady Gatorettes. Misty Dawn…"

"Really? Someone would actually name their child Misty Dawn? Really?"

I just nodded and kept on talking. "Misty Dawn is the only one who is sort of missing."

"What do you mean sort of missing?"

"Well, she's been spotted throughout the county but law enforcement hasn't been able to find her to pick her up for questioning in the murders of Bobby Derlicter, Buddy Walker, and Happy Jack Canaday.

"The Fish Florida Resort is on track to open in a couple of months and basically life's good in Po'thole and River County."

A few more minutes on live television and it was over. I had just turned my cell phone back on when it rang. Yes, I changed the ring tone from "Living on a Prayer" by Bon Jovi, to "So What" by Pink. It summed up my feelings.

"Hello."

"Thanks for not ratting me out." *Click.*

I smiled. Misty Dawn was alive and well. I also didn't have to worry about her hunting me down and making me number four on her murder list.

The phone rang again.

"Parker, we need to talk about you coming back to Po'thole for the Full Moon Crappie Festival Old Fashion Antique Show and Sale."

It was the invitation from Gracie Blanche that had started everything.

"Well, Gracie Blanche…."

About The Author

Sharon started A Dose of Nice as a three-page joke for some friends many years ago. Sporadically working on it over the course of several years and it still wasn't finished, Sharon was hauled up before her friendly tribunal of friends who demanded that she finish the book or they would have nothing to do with her.

Pushing the envelope to determine if they would hold true to their word and disbar her from their friendship, Sharon discovered they were serious. The book was finished within six months and her friends welcomed her back into the fold.

Sharon has written over one thousand magazine articles, five non-fiction books, and ghostwritten five more.

Be sure to visit www.SharonEBuck.com[1] and find out what's next on the horizon for Sharon, Parker Bell, and the Lady Gatorettes.

As always, if you have something really nice to say, publish it everywhere on the Internet. If you are unhappy, please email me directly Sharon@SharonEBuck.com and don't say anything bad on review websites.

Sharon is available for speaking engagements and doing webinars for reader and writer groups.

---

1.   http://www.SharonEBuck.com

Go to SharonEBuck.com, sign up for my newsletter, and get your FREE

Acknowledgements

Books are never written alone. There are many people who cross our lives at different points in time and who consciously or subconsciously impact our lives in one form or another. I thank every colorful character I have ever come across and, being a Southerner, I've come across a boatload of them!

"Thank you" doesn't began to cover my gratitude for the hours and hours of telephone conversations with Barbara Smothers. Everyone should be so lucky to have a great friend like Barb. Without your kick in the fanny, I might never have finished this book. Thanks to Howard for his patience with all of our phone calls!

To my dear friend and editor Nancy Quatrano, thanks for your friendship, encouragement, support, and editing skills. Without you, this book would still be languishing in the deep throes of my computer. Any editing mistakes are mine.

To Jakolien Sok, thanks for getting me back on track on writing A Dose of Nice. I appreciate your friendship. Thanks to Arjan Warmerdam for the hours on Skype with Jakolien. Many good laughs.

To Jodi Sykes, Allegra Kitchens, Linda Nipper, Margaret Zahner, Florida Writers Association Ancient City Chapter, and Florida Sisters in Crime, thanks for making me laugh and all of your encouragement, I appreciate it!

And, lastly, to Plop-Plop, Angel (2), and Sox – thanks for making me realize I can't sit behind the computer all day long and not play with you. Thanks for making me get up and have some fun!

Ever and always, thanks be to God – who deserves all of the glory.

About the Author

True confession time. I have a wicked sense of humor in case you hadn't noticed. My true desire and hope is that I made you laugh while reading this book. My mission is to change the world with laughter one book at a time.

I write the Florida Parker Bell humorous mystery series featuring the Lady Gatorettes. Florida crazy isn't just for tourists, the natives are unique in their own special way. Those zany folks who who live in northeast Florida can't quite make up their minds if they belong in Florida or south Georgia. They do believe in having a good time along with some mayhem, mischief, murder, and wackiness thrown in there. My laugh-out-loud books are clean with no cursing or graphic sex. Read them today!

I grew up in Palatka, Florida, traveled the Southeast extensively for a number of years, and currently reside in Jacksonville, Florida. I decided for my health and well-being it was better to live elsewhere once people in my hometown realized the Parker Bell Cozy Mystery series is loosely (very loosely, according to my attorney) based on them.

When I'm not doing my favorite thing...writing...I enjoy walking her little rescue dog, traveling, reading books, and cracking my friends up with funny stories and my sense of humor.

Read more at https://SharonEBuck.com.

www.ingramcontent.com/pod-product-compliance
Lightning Source LLC
Chambersburg PA
CBHW051209160726
47994CB00002B/529